THIS STRANGE WAY
of DYING

STORIES OF MAGIC, DESIRE AND THE FANTASTIC

THIS STRANGE WAY
of DYING

SILVIA MORENO-GARCIA

singular fiction, poetry, nonfiction, translation, drama, and graphic books

Library and Archives Canada Cataloguing in Publication

Moreno-Garcia, Silvia, author
    This strange way of dying : stories of magic, desire and the
fantastic / Silvia Moreno-Garcia.

ISBN 978-1-55096-354-0 (pbk.)

    I. Title.

PS8626.O7427S87 2013   C813'.6   C2013-902876-5

Design and Composition by Michael Callaghan / Cover Art by Sara Diesel
Typeset in Fairfield, Trajan, and Constantia fonts at Moons of Jupiter Studios

Published by Exile Editions Ltd ~ www.ExileEditions.com
144483 Southgate Road 14 – GD, Holstein, Ontario, N0G 2A0

We gratefully acknowledge the Canada Council for the Arts, the Government of Canada,
the Ontario Arts Council, and Ontario Creates for their support toward our
publishing activities.

Canadian sales representation: The Canadian Manda Group, 664 Annette Street,
Toronto ON M6S 2C8 www.mandagroup.com 416 516 0911

North American and international distribution, and U.S. sales:
Independent Publishers Group, 814 North Franklin Street,
Chicago IL 60610 www.ipgbook.com toll free: 1 800 888 4741

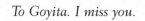

To Goyita. I miss you.

Contents

SCALES AS PALE AS MOONLIGHT

A child wailed in the dark, in the scrubland.

The serpent screams like that as it waits in the thickets.

Laura opened the window and stood still, listening. The cry did not repeat itself. She shouldn't have listened to the stories her aunts were telling about the *alicante*, how it would come in the middle of the night, into the homes where nursing women slept. It crept over stones and grass and into the bedroom, and it sucked the mother's milk. Sometimes, if the baby of the family woke up, the snake placed the tip of its tail in the infant's mouth, pacifying it so it would not stir the mother.

Silly stories and superstitions she'd heard as a child.

But she had no baby. No child clung to her breast.

Outside, there were only the trees and the dark.

※

The women were making tortillas, palming the dough into shape. This day there was no talk of snakes that steal milk.

Laura wished for rain.

She wished she'd gone with Hector.

He was hunting with some of her other cousins, off to find deer and snakes. She'd hunted with him when they were kids, using a two-pronged stick to catch the snakes; afterwards, they'd splash in the *jagüel*. He was the one closest to her. The rest of them, the cousins and the aunts and uncles, they looked at her kindly, but she knew what they thought of her, they thought she had gone weak in the city. City girl with no mettle, no strength in her hollow bones. The women started roasting chilis and the smell tickled Laura's nostrils, making her cough. Like the snakes, which flee when you burn chilis at night to keep them at bay, far from the low, warm bedrolls where the country folk sleep. Laura slid away from the house, away from the quiet stares of her aunts.

The town had only one store. It sold everything from batteries to canned goods. At dusk, the children gathered outside of it, to drink pop and chew bubble gum.

Laura went in and rummaged at the magazine rack – pictures of pop and soap opera stars in garish colours on the cover. The owner had tossed some used comic books, two pulp novels and a romance novel into the stack.

The romance novel was an old Gothic story, with the heroine standing, pop-eyed, in front of an ominous castle.

Laura approached the counter. The woman behind it was very pregnant, her belly straining against the confines of her blouse, sweat dripping down her brow.

The shopkeeper smiled.

"Only this," Laura said, placing the book upon the counter and when the shopkeeper opened her mouth to speak, Laura cut her off. "I have exact change."

Laura placed the money on the counter and felt the accusing eyes of the woman as she left the store.

She went back to the house but stayed outside, sitting under the shade of a pepper tree. She read about the Gothic heroine, who had married a rich man and now lived in his accursed castle, riddled with dozens of secret passages. The heroine had fallen into a pit of poisonous pythons. Laura thought it was ridiculous. Pythons are not poisonous. Neither is the *alicante*, the corn snake, moving through the maize field, hiding in the furrows. *Pituophis deppei deppei.* She'd looked it up in an encyclopedia, in the days when taxonomy and animals had fascinated her.

She read about the silly heroine, who suspected the castle was haunted by the ghost of her husband's previous wife, until the sun started going down and the rumble of a truck made her lift her eyes.

In the brush, she thought she saw something moving, a shadow disappearing. Probably not a snake, though there were plenty up the hill, in the little cemetery.

She walked into the house just as her cousins came in carrying a few rabbits and laughing, chattering; the dogs wagged their tails and sniffed around their feet.

Laura sat on a chair and watched.

"Laura, I caught a snake. A large one," Hector said when he saw her.

Snake meat. Pale, soft meat. They'd serve it next day, together with the rabbit. She'd eaten lots of dry rattlesnake meat the year she broke her left arm, because they said it would help it heal faster.

"No deer?" she asked, not because she was interested in the answer, but because it was customary. A ritual.

"Nah," Hector said and shifting, noticing her far-off look, he spoke again. "Wanna have a cigarette?"

They stood outside, leaning against the wall. Hector was down to his last smoke, so they had to share, like the teenagers they'd once been. Laura took a drag and handed the cigarette back to Hector.

"What's up?"

"I talked to Rolando yesterday."

"What did he say?"

"The usual," Laura muttered.

It had all been very polite, almost scripted.

Rolando blamed her, hated her. Two times blood and child had seeped out of her body during the first trimester and then the child, the one baby she'd birthed, was a cold lump which spilled onto the doctor's hands.

"He thinks I should stay."

"You want to go back to the city?"

"What is there to do here?" she asked in exasperation.

"You bored?"

Laura did not reply. It was not as much being bored as being fed up. With everything and everyone.

"I can take you to dinner in Calera tomorrow night," he said. "We can go to a nightclub afterwards."

"There's a nightclub in Calera?"

"The guy who owns the hotel has a little annex, right in the hotel, and it serves as a nightclub. If we go early we can walk around the church and catch a movie."

"Did they ever put air conditioning in the movie theatre?"

"You wish."

She took the cigarette back, nodding.

X

Her cousin was right. The cinema had the same old ratty seats and was as hot as an oven, packed to the brim on Saturday. Fifteen years had added some grime to the floor, leaving the rest untouched. They caught a matinee and then went to the church. Laura stared up at the pale icon of the Virgin, a porcelain child in her arms.

Dinner was at a little restaurant with sunflowers painted on the walls and Hector topped it all by dragging her to the promised nightclub.

It was small, stuffy. Hector danced with a woman in a tight yellow shirt. She watched them, feeling jealous that they could be that young, forgetting Hector was twenty-nine, only a year her junior.

On the drive back she pretended to sleep. The drinks had only made her more miserable. Laura pressed her face against the window and glimpsed a pale snake on the side of the road. White as snow and rather large, unlike the snakes they'd chased through the cemetery.

"Hector, look," she said.

"Huh?" he asked.

They passed it by. She looked at the rearview mirror and saw only darkness.

✺

Laura woke up late. She had a cup of *atole* and wondered if it might rain. There were no umbrellas in the house and she'd be taking a chance if she went up to the old cemetery.

She decided to take the walk, what the hell. It might do her good.

They didn't like to let her do this. To walk alone. It was what had gotten her into trouble with Rolando. She'd begun to walk out at nights. She'd take off and walk and walk through Mexico City. No coat. One time, no shoes. It worried him, of course. All the insecurity and Laura out there. He'd sent her to stay with her relatives after the last time, when she had fallen asleep at an underpass and the cops had found her.

The grass in the cemetery tickled her knees. She pressed her hands against a familiar headstone.

She had spent many afternoons playing there with her cousin before moving to the city to live with her dad. She had hunted *alicantes* with Hector. It was a scary creature, but she was brave back then; she did not fear the snake though she'd heard tales that it might grow ten metres long.

She wasn't brave anymore. She wasn't the girl in the photographs, holding snakeskins across her legs. The tough girl who could ride better than all the boys, who helped her uncle with his taxidermy.

She was this sad, dark, pitiable thing running in the night.

A cry, like a child's, made her raise her head. Neck tense, eyes wide, Laura looked around, trying to determine where the sound had come from.

There was a rustle in the grass and she rushed forward, but there was nothing there.

The cry did not repeat itself.

⋊

Laura found the old encyclopedia. The fan in her room screeched. The rains would come soon and cool the house. She might turn the fan off then and sit listening to the patter of the raindrops.

She looked at the pictures of snakes in the old volumes. Turning a page she found scraps of paper. Drawings of winged serpents. It was Hector's handiwork.

She stared at the knotted snakes and his messy handwriting. There was also a Polaroid of them. Laura had pigtails. Hector was missing two front teeth. She smiled.

And here now, another photograph. This one was older: Laura's mother and Laura by her side, a toddler. In the mother's arms a baby. Laura's brother. She'd been three when he died in the crib. Her mother killed herself four months later. Father had sent Laura to live in the countryside, with her grandmother. She'd gone back to Mexico City only when he had remarried a bountiful stepmother who gave him six kids.

Laura felt her insides knotting themselves, like a piece of string. It was one thing to walk by her mother's grave, but it was another to stare at her photograph. They were so much alike. Same dark, large eyes. Their thin mouths both curled in an uncertain smile. The frail neck.

She grabbed the Gothic paperback, hoping its melodramatic scenes would calm her down, but now it was turning into a Jane Eyre rip-off, with a mad wife stashed in the tunnels.

Laura turned off the lights.

※

"Do you remember those stories about *alicantes* Mama Dolores used to tell us?" Laura asked.

Hector was taking out sweet bread from a paper bag and putting it on a platter for dinner. He shrugged.

"What part?"

"That old *alicantes* can be very large and long. They grow fur and wings sprout from their backs."

"Ah, yes."

"Have you ever seen a large one?"

"How large are you thinking? I've certainly never seen one with fur or wings."

"We helped your dad stuff the dead animals, remember? We used marbles for the eyes of snakes."

"For the eyes of everything."

"They felt very real. The eyes."

Hector folded the bag and left it on the kitchen table. He offered her a plate and a piece of sugary bread.

"What did you do with the mounted animals?" she asked.

"I gave them away. They reminded me too much of dad."

"Did it work?"

They painted the baby's room yellow and removed the wallpaper with the little dancing elephants. Threw away the crib. It did not help. She still woke in the middle of the night expecting the cry of an infant that never came.

"I suppose. I still miss him."

Laura nibbled the bread without any appetite. She knew they wanted her to eat well. She tried to comply, the same way she tried to meet the others for all the meals even though she disliked these gatherings. Her aunts disapproved when she woke late. Townsfolk wake early, with the dawn. Her tendency to roll out of bed close to noon was proof of her decadence. Of what the city had done to her.

"I was at the cemetery. I stopped by my mother's grave and put some wildflowers there. I left some for your dad too."

"You walked all the way there?"

"It's not that far," she replied. "Only half an hour's walk. I'm not an invalid."

"You shouldn't have gone by yourself."

Hector looked at her with kind, understanding eyes. She disliked his pity.

"Do you have a beer?" she asked.

They sat outside, on the back steps, watching the moon rise, huge and round, as they drank.

X

Rolando used to phone thrice a week. The calls had diminished in frequency.

This time he didn't bother making an excuse, no stuff about being busy with work. He sounded irritated. He hung up quickly. Laura tapped her nails against the telephone and went back to her room and her book. She had not finished the paperback. It sat by her bed, like a venomous creature waiting to attack.

She sat, cross-legged, in the middle of her bed, smoking a cigarette. Rolando didn't like it when she smoked and she stopped the first time she got pregnant, but Rolando wasn't there and Laura had no children.

Don Quijote bored her to tears and she stretched a hand towards the paperback. It was only a silly story. Snake pits, for God's sake. She'd been brave. Where was that bravery now?

Laura opened the book. The previous wife was not only insane, but now the husband had planned to drive this second one mad and also stash her in the tunnels.

There was talk of bricking her alive into a wall. Shades of Poe.

This time the cry was so loud it seemed to be coming from within the house.

Laura jumped to her feet and opened the window.

The trees were ink black, brush and wilderness extending behind the house. It was dark, but moonlight made it shine, the opalescent skin almost glowing. A large, white snake.

Laura grabbed a sweater and hurried to the back door. She opened the door, the chill, night air hitting her in the face. She walked around the house, looking for the snake.

It was gone.

⚮

"I heard a baby crying outside," she told Hector. "I think it was a snake."

"Snakes don't cry."

They sat behind the house, under a tree. It was hot but a cool breeze blew, ruffling her hair. She'd thought of going for a swim in the *jagüel*, damn the rains that refused to visit them, but Hector didn't want to go and he wouldn't let her venture there by herself, on account of the leeches living in the water.

She thought it was an excuse. Hector was always near, helpful and kind, but she'd begun to resent him.

She felt a prisoner, unable to go into town on her own, sneaking out if she wanted to take a walk – but now even that was difficult and he was keeping a better eye on her. She hadn't been able to visit the cemetery again. He wouldn't let her go. It would be sad, he said, remembering all that stuff. Death and dying.

As though she'd forgotten.

"I'm going in. I want to phone Rolando," she said.

Hector began to protest. She ignored him and grabbed the heavy, Bakelite telephone sitting in the living room. It rang a dozen times, but nobody answered. She sat with the telephone on her lap.

She thought of the heroine in the castle, waking to discover she'd been buried alive inside the walls of the great manor.

※

They went to the *tianguis* in Calera on Saturday. Laura and Hector walked down the rows of stalls carrying a large canvas bag, looking at the merchants selling fruits, vegetables, meat and clothes.

She stopped in front of a merchant with toys and *alebrijes* on display. The bright, multicoloured paper mache creatures were a mix of different animals. Fish with tails. Bats with feathers. One was a coiled, winged snake. She picked it up, letting it rest on the palm of her hand.

"Do you want it?" Hector asked.

"No, it's fine," Laura said, putting it down and wiping her fingers against her shirt.

"You were up last night. Outside the house."

She had been but only for a few minutes. The fan whirred inside her room, noisy. It was stifling hot. She needed the cool night air.

"Were you spying on me?"

"You woke me up. The door banged open. Have you been taking your medication?"

She knew the look on his face. It was the same look Rolando had when he glanced at her: distrust. She remembered the birthing pains and the last push. The room, so still and quiet. No child's wail emerging from the tiny child. And he … all he'd said was *ah*. As though he'd expected it all along. Laura couldn't be trusted with anything. Laura with her sadness and her moods, the two miscarriages and the stillbirth, the bouts of anger. And the running. Running through the night. Just like her mother.

"Yes," Laura muttered.

She did, though they only made it worse – the sadness always there and the nervous ticks. Sometimes she'd turn in her bed and think she could still feel the butterfly kicks of the child in her womb and she pressed her fingers tight against her stomach only to feel nothing.

And she ran.

"Are you sure? Maybe you forgot."

"What am I? Five?" she asked. "Damn it, I'm tired of having you counting my medication and following me around. I need to go back to Mexico City. I'll take the bus tonight."

"Look Laura, you'll do as Rolando says and he said you need to rest and take your pills. You were sounding odd last time you spoke to him."

Laura chuckled. "Have you been phoning Rolando?"

Hector gave her a guilty look, jamming his hands in his pockets. "He doesn't want you getting in trouble."

She knew the truth then, looking at him. It had been pre-arranged. The sweet, thoughtful cousin. Her childhood playmate, hired to play the nanny. A kind jailer for the mad wife. No attic for her, no bricked tunnel: just the placid, quiet little house in the little town.

"It's not some bizarre conspiracy," Hector said. "We are all worried about you. You hear snakes crying."

"You'd have believed me about the snakes when we were younger," she said.

On the way back home she clutched her paperback.

※

She'd been brave. Headstrong and fearless. Not like the heroine of the novel, never snivelling in the dark, never wavering as a candle sputtered. Hunting snakes without shivering.

This time she was ready. She went to bed dressed, shoes on, and when the cry echoed through the night she hurried quietly to the door, flashlight in hand.

She followed the sound, across a field of yellowed grass, up a hill, towards the cemetery. Laura pushed the little iron gate open and shone her flashlight, but the weeds and grass made it impossible to see well.

The cry, however, was stronger now. She was very close.

Laura stepped forward until she reached a little clearing. She saw the snake there. Large, like in the stories. Scales as pale as moonlight. No, not scales. Feathers. Soft, downy feathers and a pair of wings. The snake opened its mouth, showing its teeth. It did not recoil at the sight of the flashlight and she realized it was blind.

It must be very old.

Laura knelt down, whispering kind words. The snake slid forward, pressing its head against her hand.

Laura shushed it and began to sing a lullaby, one her mother had sang to her. The snake rested its cold head against her chest.

Laura unbuttoned her blouse and offered her breast. She knew there ought to be no milk, that she was as dry and empty as an old corn husk, yet the snake swallowed milk, fed quietly.

Laura caressed its soft skin. She brushed the tiny feathers of the ancient snake and the feathers came off, like a dandelion shedding its seeds. The feathers floated away, spread by a breeze. The snake had lost its skin.

A baby, the colour of an ivory icon, snuggled against her body, fast asleep at her breast. She cried as the first drops of rain began to splash on her face.

MAQUECH

The jewel-encrusted beetle walked slowly across the table, dragging its golden chain behind. It was bigger than any other maquech he'd ever seen before and more richly decorated.

Gerardo put down the eyeglass.

"It's not my usual purchase," he said.

"It's rare," Mario replied. "This is the last one my grandfather made before he passed away."

"Monkeys are big now. Everyone wants a monkey."

"But it doesn't need a lot of food or water," Mario protested. "That's a benefit."

"Do you think my clients worry about things like food or water? Listen, I sold five ostriches two months ago. People want large animals."

It was a lie. He sold fish and birds and maybe a reptile or two. He could not afford extravagant purchases like ostriches.

"I need the money," Mario confessed. "I want to go to Canada."

"What for?"

"I want to see the polar bears before they disappear. Before all the ice melts away."

Gerardo stared at Mario. Who the hell cared about polar bears? Unless Gerardo was importing them he didn't give a damn about them or the ice. Canada was far away and there were more pressing problems right now, like how he was going to afford that month's water bill. Up went the bill and for a small trader of exotic pets there was always competition, taxes and bribes to pay, food to buy for the animals. If he didn't sell them quickly he'd have to keep the beasts for months on end and spend tons of money on their care.

And then Mario came and talked about looking at polar bears? Christ on the cross. They were probably better off without so many of them anyway. He tried to calculate the amount of food one of those things must devour each month and shook his head.

"Look, I can't give you much," Gerardo said.

※

Gerardo put the maquech in the terrarium together with the bits of wood Mario had given him. The maquech fed on the bacteria of decomposing wood, so at least it wouldn't cost too much to maintain. He recalled the piranhas he'd bought last May. Hungry, ugly little things. He wouldn't make that mistake again.

Gerardo looked at the maquech and wondered who might buy this one. He'd seen people wearing a maquech on their lapel or their dress but usually they had tacky plastic faux-jewels on their backs. This little insect had been painted and decorated with semi-precious stones. It was not a cheap bug and he needed to make a good sale.

He went through his list of regular clients, discarded all of them and kept coming back to a single name: Arturo de la Vega.

He'd never sold anything to Arturo but if there was a buyer in Mexico City it was Arturo. He was disgustingly rich. While everyone else was worrying about getting running water that week, how to purchase a kilo of tortillas, the eternally high levels of pollution and the assholes trying to express-kidnap you, Arturo spent insane amounts of money on exotic pets. Arturo de la Vega had a roof garden with a pool and palm trees in a city where people ran behind the water trucks, filling barrels and *tinajas* twice a week. Arturo de la Vega drove a car when everyone else had to walk, or at best be carried on a litter down Reforma.

If you managed to sell an animal to Arturo de la Vega you were in the big leagues.

But Gerardo had never sold a thing to him. He was too small, too unknown, too much of a provincial newcomer.

He drummed his fingers against the table.

He took out the camera and snapped a few pictures of the maquech.

※

He normally did not dream. There was no space in the cramped apartment for dreams, filled with the stench of the birds and fish.

That night he dreamt of rivers and quiet, dark places where the sunlight turns green with the colour of the trees.

※

Three days later the monthly offering period for Arturo de la Vega opened up. It was only a one-day window and Gerardo had to line up outside the reception office for many hours prior to that. He stood baking under the furious sun and watched a man with cages strapped behind his back walk by. Mechanical owls blinked their multicoloured eyes at Gerardo and shook their metal wings. There was a water seller across the street yelling the same litany over and over again.

"Water. Fresh, pure water."

He closed his eyes, thinking of a stream's murmur.

Somebody shoved him forward and Gerardo snapped his eyes open and walked forward, one more step towards the building's entrance. A long time later he stepped into the lobby and placed his submission package, nothing more than a few snapshots and an introduction letter, on the narrow cedar table.

Then it was back to his apartment, down three flights of stairs. He couldn't afford a floor above ground with a glass window, not even a window with metal shutters. Sunlight was costly.

Gerardo fed the fish and the birds first. Then he turned to the maquech.

The insect walked from one end of its terrarium to the other.

"What are you thinking?" he asked the maquech.

The maquech stood very still.

Gerardo stood still too.

He didn't talk to the animals. It was not his thing to coo and smile and babble over an animal like it was a baby. He fed them. He housed them. He sold them. That was it.

Nothing less and nothing more.

※

It was water day. Four hours of running water. The luxury of a warm shower was something he looked forward to the whole week. He hummed and closed his eyes and thought of blue-green waterfalls.

As he stood in the shower, head bowed under the spray, he heard a loud pounding.

He wrapped a towel around his waist and opened the door.

A courier held out a letter for him.

"From Mr. de la Vega," the man said.

Gerardo tore open the black envelope. Inside was a card with an address and a date. An invitation to Mr. de la Vega's apartment. An invitation to show him the maquech.

He'd done it.

He was going to de la Vega's home, to parade his maquech in front of him like a real trader.

Gerardo froze as he realized the wooden or plastic cages where he normally stuffed his merchandise wouldn't suffice. He needed something grand and elegant that would display the maquech like an elaborate brooch.

Perhaps a red velvet box lined in silk with appropriate breathing holes. At once he began to panic, considering the price of this custom-made, urgent item.

But then he looked at the maquech with its golden chain, the painted back, the tiny stones in the centre of the composition. A breathing mosaic. A walking jewel. It was beautiful. It needed a beautiful setting.

※

The room was black and bright as polished obsidian, the floor and the walls reflected and distorted Gerardo's image as he opened the box and held it up for de la Vega to inspect.

The young man glanced at the maquech, just a little glance and looked up at him.

"What on earth is that?"

"*Zopherus chilensis*," Gerardo said. "In Yucatan they call them maquech and wear them as a brooch."

"It's alive?"

"Yes. Live jewelry. It is decorated with…"

"Pablo, did you select this?"

A man in impeccable white wearing a matching white hat stepped from behind de la Vega's right, a little silver tablet in his left hand.

"Yes," said the man.

"What for?"

"It's a curiosity. I haven't seen one since I was a child."

"It's ugly," de la Vega said and waved Gerardo away.

＊

He considered tearing off the jewels from the insect's back. There were bills to pay and the maquech had been an extravagant purchase at a time when he couldn't afford it. Not that Gerardo could ever afford much.

"Stupid, slow bug," he told the maquech as it walked on the palm of his hand. Or maybe not stupid, merely indifferent. In Yucatan they said it could live for many decades, even centuries. Maybe after hundreds of years walking in the jungle things such as humans and their games were of little importance. Of course these were just legends. Stories old people tell. He didn't believe them.

But as the maquech began to crawl up his arm he thought what time might be like for a quasi-immortal creature, sitting under the jade shade of the trees.

※

Gerardo was thinking of black eyeless fish and sacred waterholes when the phone rang. The waterholes melted away as he punched a key.

"Yes?" he asked.

"It's Pablo, Mr. de la Vega's assistant. I need you to come tomorrow to the apartment and bring your insect again. He wants to have a second look at it."

Pablo's voice had a hint of metal as it poured from the phone, crisp and sharp and bright. Gerardo swallowed and leaned forward.

"I'm sorry?"

"Tomorrow at five. You got that?"

"Yeah, sure."

"See you then."

Gerardo punched another key. He sat back. The maquech took a step with each tick of the black minute hand of the clock on the wall. The heavy jewels on its back made it slow. Or maybe it did not care to move quickly. There was all the time in the world for it to reach its destination.

X

Pablo, the man in white, was wearing grey this time. His fingers danced over the tablet and he spoke with his measured voice.

"They use them as love talismans. The Mayans said there was a girl that was turned into that insect."

"The Mayans thought a princess' doomed lover was turned into a maquech so he could remain close to her heart," Gerardo said, correcting the assistant. "The Mayans thought it was a symbol of immortality."

Pablo glanced up at him, his fingers frozen for a second.

Arturo de la Vega did not reply. He sat in his obsidian room, holding a glass between his fingers. He did not look at the insect that Gerardo was holding up in its velvet box for him to examine. Instead, Arturo set down his glass on top of a black, lacquered table.

"I don't enjoy insects," he said. "I don't find them interesting. They're too small, too common, and they don't live very long."

"A maquech can live three or four years in captivity. Maybe even more with the proper care."

"That's not very long."

"Do you purchase your animals based on their longevity?"

"Normally longevity is not an issue."

"Four years is not a short period of time."

"It seems short to me."

"Then you shouldn't have called me. I can't make it live forty years just for your sake," he said, and he knew it was a rude remark but he could not help himself. Arturo had made him wait for two hours before he deigned to see him and he was tired, with this curious sensation of levity, as though everything that might happen was inconsequential.

"Do you smoke?" Arturo asked as he took out a white gold case and plucked a thin black cigarette.

"Sure," Gerardo said, although he had not smoked in over five years. He couldn't afford it.

Arturo made a little motion with his hand and Pablo stepped forward, lighting their cigarettes. Up close, Pablo's eyes glinted a synthetic blue-silver. Modified. Beautified.

Arturo puffed twice and smiled.

"I'm not completely indifferent to your beetle, Gerardo. But I'm not completely interested either. I've got other traders showing their goods to me and they have very impressive merchandise and they are much better known than you. Does he come recommended?"

"No recommendations," Pablo said with his beautiful, beautiful voice and Gerardo wondered if that too had been modified. "But talent springs from the oddest place."

"I do have a knack for spotting talent," Arturo said.

"Mr. de la Vega made Yuko Saitou an overnight sensation. Her two-headed koi are all the rage."

"Synthets," Gerardo said.

"We buy many, many things."

There was a pause. The smoke of the cigarettes curled up, towards the glass ceiling and Gerardo shifted his weight, feeling suddenly pinned under the men's gaze.

"How about a test?" Pablo asked.

"I'm sorry?"

"Try on the beetle. Wear it."

"That's not such a bad idea," de la Vega said.

"Now?"

"I have a party on Friday. Come back Friday. We'll see how it goes."

※

The maquech smelled like old wood. Beneath its jewels it was the colour of wood and if Gerardo closed his eyes it felt like it was a leaf moving upon his hand, stirred by the breeze.

He opened his eyes and let the beetle back into its terrarium. He turned on the TV and clicked through the channels and there was the news and talk about crime rates, and the soap operas, and the late night variety hour pop-star sensation.

Gerardo tried to concentrate on the TV and the images flickered in dazzling colour but seemed as insubtantial as ghosts. There was nothing remotely interesting to watch inside his box of an apartment with its concrete lid.

He turned off the TV and sat in silence.

He thought he could hear the rain falling, far away.

⁂

A woman walked with a leopard on a leash, a teenage boy wore a snakeskin jacket and a real snake around his neck. Men wrapped in silk and feathers with fish scales glued to their faces drank out of amethyst glasses. Women in dresses made of iridescent butterfly wings smiled at him.

And then, among the sea of revellers, Arturo walked forth with a jaguar's skull upon his head and a cape made of animal bones and he smiled at Gerardo. Pablo, black suit and black hat, served as his shadow.

"So good to see you. So good. Are you having fun?" Arturo asked.

"It's a very grand party."

"It is. Have you brought it then?"

Gerardo opened the velvet box and held it up. Pablo slipped forward and took the box, took the maquech, and placed it upon Arturo's shirt, fastening the golden chain. It shone like a star. It shone brighter than he'd ever seen it before, as if to please Gerardo, and people circled Arturo and fawned and sighed.

Pablo, who was still next to Gerardo, smiled a tiny, calculated smile.

"Will he buy it?" Gerardo asked as the star moved away and was lost from his sight.

"He never knows what he wants," Pablo said. "But he likes real things and real things are scarce."

Gerardo was quiet and then Pablo took out his tablet and walked away. "Luck of the draw," he said, without turning to look at him.

※

A couple of hours later Pablo walked to Gerardo and handed him a card.

"Mr. de la Vega wishes to purchase your beetle."

Gerardo nodded. He did not know what else one was supposed to do in such situations.

"Come back sometime," Pablo said.

"The maquech," Gerardo muttered. Pablo's blue eyes swept over him, a question mark. "It'll need to eat. There's some wood it needs."

"I'll send someone."

He was escorted out of the party, to a black car with tinted windows. He had never been in a car. Well, nothing like a real car. Once he had sat in his uncle's beat-up *bochito* when he was a kid but he hardly remembered anything about that ride.

Now he went down Reforma, down the only car lane, fast like a silver bullet. And he thought he'd never, ever forget that moment.

X

Gerardo walked down three flights of stairs into his windowless apartment.

There was something missing there. But everything seemed to be in its place, all the papers remained where he'd left them, each bird sat in its cage, each fish swam in its tank.

When he walked into the kitchen he saw ants were feasting on a sandwich he had left on the table and he tossed it in the garbage.

He turned on the TV and there was a report about riots due to increases in the cost of the tortilla. Somewhere in Santa Julia two men had been shot for stealing hoarded water. In the colonia Roma, Mexican freshwater turtles were being served as appetizers at a fine restaurant. He turned it off.

There was something missing.

He grabbed the terrarium and started putting the pieces of wood into a bag so he could courier them to de la Vega. And as he did he realized what was missing:

the smell of old wood and jungle. The smell of the maquech.

That night Gerardo did not dream of rivers.

.

STORIES WITH
HAPPY ENDINGS

... and I said "But what's a vampire doing in Mexico City?"

The vampire was eating meatballs at a late-night restaurant and smoking cheap cigarettes that tinted the fingers and defiled the tongue.

He spoke with his mouth full, bits of meatball tumbling down to his plate. "Twenty million people."

Behind him, through the window, I could see two street kids hanging by the cars and I was afraid of getting my tires slashed yet again. On the other side of the street I spotted the local beggar, palm outstretched and a baby upon his knee. In the ten years I had lived in the area, I had seen ten different babies. A new one every time the other started toddling. I had never given him a dime. Such stuff is for the tourists.

"Do you drink blood?"

"I drink pain."

"Sounds fun."

"You live off the same thing," he said, pointing to the audio recorder which sat between us.

"That's a very archaic view of journalists," I said.

I thought of my beat, which is crime, and the eerie beauty of photographing the corpses the night has to give, a solitary candle burning by the body. Splatters of blood on the pavement and the click of the camera.

I miss the days of silver nitrate and dark rooms. Of enlargers and red lights. We've lost a slice of reality with the advent of digital cameras. Everything looks more distant, hazier, when it's composed of jumbled pixels.

The waitress wandered by, refilling my cup of coffee. She looked tired. Like she pulled double shifts and slept three hours in between jobs.

"Where do you work?"

"Security guard at a hosiery factory," he said, pressing his cigarette against the ashtray. "Night shift. Today's my day off."

"No castle?"

I looked at my pad and my doodles of bats and fangs stark upon the lined paper.

"In this fucking economy?" he asked.

"If I was an immortal vampire I'd try harder."

"Necessity."

I spooned two sugars into my cup, then added a third for good measure. Slow nights always mean an extra sugar and the chance to talk to whoever is sitting at the cafés and restaurants, to perhaps pull another kind of story out of the hat. That's how I'd found him. My usual curiosity. We started chatting, he said he was a vampire, I placed my recorder on the table. And yes, I've heard weirder stories. More bizarre confessions. Midnight is a time to talk to strangers, to unload your gut in between cigarettes.

"Any super powers? Turn into mist? Seduce people with your eyes?"

He just laughed. Not much to look at. Young guy. Bad haircut and a cheap shirt. Poor teeth. But his hands were long and thin and beautiful. Hands fit for Germán Robles, who played the most famous Mexican vampire back in '57; hands to beckon his acolytes of the night.

He also had a good voice. Smooth and low. That might have been just the cigarettes scratching the vocal folds, but it sounded elegant. It was the voice which had drawn me to his table. He had raised his hand and said "hey" to the waitress and I'd turned my head to search for the source of the sound. I saw him. He looked at me with dark, deep eyes and smiled. His teeth were bad so the smile didn't have quite the same effect as the voice, but I grabbed my camera and sat with him.

If only he hadn't stained the fingers yellow with the cigarettes. If only he didn't have the dark circles under his eyes. If only... then he might have played Karol de Lavud and appeared on my television set on Sundays, like when I was a kid.

"How old are you?"

"Not sure," he said, pressing a finger against his chin and thinking. "Probably a hundred by now. I've lost track."

"You've lost the Transylvanian accent."

"I also pawned the coffin."

"I pawned the TV last summer."

"Got it back?"

"No. Only shit on it, anyway. I like to read."

"Newspapers?"

"Stories about detectives who solve crimes," I said. "Stories with happy endings."

"I don't read."

"Nobody does anymore. That's why journalism doesn't pay."

We were two archaisms sharing a table and drinking coffee. The journalist and the vampire, both made irrelevant by a faster than fast life; smartphones, hundreds of TV channels on Cablevision, porn on demand and Wikipedia. Modernity was sharper than a stake and the moors had been drained to make way for condos.

"Any vampire brides?"

"I can't afford to go on dates."

"Any Renfields?"

"Why? You looking for a new job?"

He slid his thin, long hands into a shirt pocket and pulled out his crumpled pack of cigarettes. He lit one. I almost wanted to grab his hand and slap it. Damn nicotine ruining his skin.

Stained hands toyed with the match he'd just used.

The cigarette glowed like a single, unblinking eye. Like a will-o'-the-wisp.

I stared at him and to tell the truth, I was a bit hypnotized by the whole tableau. The hunched shoulders, the jacket and the aquiline face.

My phone rang and I grabbed the pad, scribbling quickly. I drank my coffee in one big gulp.

"I've got a thing to cover," I said.

It felt good to be able to stretch my legs out of that booth and sling the camera over my shoulder. To palm my keys and make sure they were in the usual place. Murder awaited outside, and the cops and the group of onlookers, curious about what had happened.

"Are you going to do a story about me?" he asked.

"There's not much of a story," I replied.

"Alright," he said, looking dejected.

He grabbed a napkin, wrote a number on it and handed it to me.

"If you ever want to learn more about vampires, call me."

I left the money by my empty cup and stepped out.

Later, near dawn, I drove back home. The prostitutes lining the avenue were starting to disperse. In some streets you can buy a whore for fifty pesos. The same as a few beers or three *tortas*.

On a corner, I saw the vampire standing there with one hand in his pocket and the other holding his cigarette. He looked shy of one hundred under the harsh light of the streetlamp.

I thought of the city as a hooker with her neck pulsating, offering all its misery and pain for the taking.

Then I veered left, leaving the avenue behind, slipping into smaller, narrower streets of quiet apartment buildings.

I lost the number and I've never seen him back at the restaurant, but sometimes I wonder about vampires walking the streets late at night, going into convenience stores to buy packs of cheap cigarettes.

And the funny thing is, I never even asked for his name. And it's OK, because I'm pretty sure it wasn't Karol de Lavud and that, unlike Germán Robles, he didn't own a carriage. And I like to think of him the other way, like in the movies that ran on Sundays. All tall and skinny and swathed in a cape, defying the vampire killers...

Bed of
Scorpions

The maid brushed the two scorpions off the bed and crushed them under the heavy heel of her shoe when they fell to the floor.

"You have to check the bed every morning," the maid said. "Check your boots. They tend to get in there too. And give a good shake to your clothes. The dangerous scorpions are not the black ones. The pale ones are the ones you can miss if you're too hasty."

Beatriz stared at the white sheets.

"Have a good night."

The maid closed the door, and Beatriz was alone. She approached the large bed in the centre of the room very slowly. She peeked under the covers, afraid the maid had missed an arachnid.

Beatriz went to sleep fearing she would wake up to the sharp sting of the scorpion.

※

Beatriz rose early and found Ramon in the dining room. He seemed happy and untroubled, picking at some eggs. A shaggy, ugly dog roamed around the table. It made her nervous.

"Good morning. You want some chocolate? I can recommend it. But stay away from the solids. The cook has no talent and the—"

"I thought he'd be here this morning."

Ramon shrugged and lifted his fork. A piece of egg fell to the ground, and the dog gobbled it up.

"It's rude."

"There's plenty of time to meet and greet."

"Well, of course. Why should you care?"

"Beatriz, don't start with that. It'll spoil breakfast. Sit down."

"He didn't send an automobile like he promised, and the house is old and ugly and shabby, and there are scorpions in the beds."

"Fine," Ramon said, his hands falling on the table, making the cutlery rattle. "We'll get on the train and to hell with everything. We spent all that time and money for nothing. All those dresses and hats and now we're back worse than where we started."

She didn't tell him they were always worse off. They would swindle and cheat and steal, but money evaporated from their hands, and then it was time to start over again.

Beatriz bit her lip and was silent.

"Come on, sit."

"I'm not hungry."

"Beatriz," he began.

She did not pause for his apology.

҉

In Mexico City, they had a little courtyard with pretty potted flowers, a fountain and canaries in their cages. But that was long ago and far away. In Durango, there was nothing. Or rather, there was a sea of weeds growing as high as her knee all around the property and insects buzzing next to her ear. A dirt trail led her towards some trees and a makeshift family cemetery with small headstones.

From there, she could get a good look at the two-storey house which seemed more unattractive in the morning light than the previous evening when they had arrived. This is not, she decided, a proper hacienda.

Her childish fantasies had conjured a magnificent mansion at the height of fashion with Parisian furnishings and a handsome husband. She ought to have known better.

Movement in the grass startled Beatriz. Looking closer, she saw a huge snake scurrying behind a tombstone. She rushed into the house and sat in her room all day long.

҉

She heard him slip under the covers, but she did not turn around, her eyes fixed on the wall.

"You're still angry?"

She felt his breath against her neck and did not move, her body coiled tight.

"Come on. Don't be mad. Don't you want to...?"

"No."

"Beatriz."

"We are in his house."

"And so what? I don't care."

"No."

Ramon fell back with a heavy sigh.

"You are insufferable."

"Leave me alone."

"Beatriz, look at me."

"I want to be alone."

She turned and stared at Ramon, but he only shrugged in the way he always did, dismissing her words. She'd found his constant shrugs charming when they were younger.

"Come, kiss me," he said.

She did, then bit his lips so hard they bled.

When he buried his face against the crook of her neck, Beatriz stared at the ceiling and wondered if scorpions would fall upon them, like the maid said they sometimes did. She thought they might blanket their bodies during the night, and when dawn arrived, they would be dead.

But in the morning she still lived, and Ramon was gone.

✕

The next day, they ate *mole*. The chicken was dry and unsavoury. After the meal, the maid said that Mr. Villanueva was still sick and would not come downstairs. As a result, Ramon and Beatriz sat in the lounge by themselves and whispered to each other.

"He'll be dead in six months," Ramon muttered.

"You think so?"

"I hope so. He's thin as a stick. At least he was when I met him at The Victoria. He never got up before noon, and when he did, he was cold or burning hot all the time, and his hands shook."

"But it's not contagious."

"I told you, no. Something in his blood."

"But what if…"

"It's fine. Don't worry. Go around the house and see if there's any interesting stuff."

She did worry. She was supposed to marry that sick man. But Ramon had concluded their conversation. He unfolded the same paper he had carried under his arm during the train ride and pretended to read it.

Beatriz left the lounge. She wandered through the hallways, noticing cracks on the checkered *azulejos*.

Finally, she slipped into what the maid described as the library. It was disappointingly small. She didn't see any "interesting" stuff, which meant anything worth pocketing. If Villanueva proved to be more difficult than Ramon had anticipated, they could steal some items to justify their trip.

She glanced at the paintings on the walls, her hands brushing the spines of the books.

They had a great library once. In a corner, there had been a large terrestrial globe, and Ramon and Beatriz used to spin it and giggle, and their fingers would fall randomly over the places in the world they would visit. But their father had been a gambler and a fool, and now they would never go anywhere.

She turned away from the books.

Something on a desk caught her eye.

It was some type of mechanical bird. It had glass wings and bright glass eyes and sat in a golden cage. When she wound it up, it began to sing, moving its tail and beak. The bird turned its head, stared at Beatriz and fell silent. The melody had concluded.

"Do you like it?"

She turned, knowing it must be him. The groom Ramon had picked for her. Some naïve fellow to marry and cheat. He had black hair, dark eyes and a plain face. He was younger than she had expected. Very young. Perhaps twenty to her eighteen years.

"It's extremely pretty," she replied.

"It belonged to my mother. It sings twenty-five different melodies."

He walked towards her, leaning on a black cane and limping slightly.

"I'm Justiniano Villanueva."

The limp, like his age, was a surprise. Her brother had said her groom was a fine gentleman, but he had not mentioned much else. Neither Villanueva nor his clothes looked very fine, though. Still, she smiled.

※

She changed into the blue dress with the floral accents and the mother-of-pearl buttons, the nicest and newest one she had. The seamstress had assured her it was the style they were wearing in France. If she married Villanueva, Ramon had promised her, they would go to France, and there she would be a great lady in silks and diamonds.

For now France was a vague dream, far from the ugly little house and its shabby lounge where they congregated. Villanueva's mongrel dog sat by his feet, and the clockwork bird, now dusted for them to admire, played a short melody.

"I'm sorry I couldn't come down earlier. I was indisposed."

"We understand."

Beatriz sat quietly as they spoke. She wondered what Ramon might have told Villanueva when they first met. She tried to picture him speaking his business talk, all fake deals and imaginary tales, and then in the midst of it leaning forward and saying, very casually of course, how he happened to have a sister.

"How do you like it? I know it's not as grand as The Victoria."

"I find it charming."

A beautiful sister who played the piano very well. A sister of marriageable age. Then some other bits of conversation, all steering him in the right direction: their father had died recently, Beatriz was very sad, Ramon worried that his business kept him away from Beatriz, she was all alone in that big house. And Villanueva probably leaned forward and wondered if both of them might not like to pay him a visit during the summer.

"Well, hopefully you're not too bored. It's a quiet house."

"We enjoy quiet, don't we?"

A trap, of course. Calculated. They had played that game before. But it had been the opposite way around: it was Ramon who married or promised marriage.

"Yes," Beatriz said, monosyllables the only form of communication she could manage at the moment.

The bird stopped playing the melody. Villanueva did not wind it up again.

⚜

Later, hidden in the sea of grass, Ramon and Beatriz sat together.

"Do you remember all those years I spent learning how to play the piano?" she asked. "Father said I simply had to learn that. Look now, there's no piano."

She pulled the grass, and let it fall to the ground.

"It scares me," she said finally.

"What?"

"That he's dying."

"Who cares?"

She turned to look at him.

"He's filthy rich, you know," Ramon said as he smoked a cigarette. Normally he wore gloves to avoid staining his fingers, but he had foregone such formalities in this remote corner of the state.

"I don't want to marry him."

"I said he was rich."

"Maybe he will not want to marry me."

"He better, and you better please him. There's more money here than we've ever had."

"Then *you* please him."

Ramon grabbed her by the jaw, fingers digging into her flesh, and pulled her forward.

"I've had my share of old, ugly bitches in my bed. Sores and wrinkles and grey hair. All to keep you fed and dressed."

"To keep *us* fed and dressed," she muttered.

He squeezed her tighter and clenched the cigarette between his teeth.

"Don't be an ungrateful little whore. You know what happens to ungrateful whores."

She blinked. She knew.

"If you bruise me, he'll notice," she whispered.

Ramon removed his hand.

"It's your turn this time," he muttered.

He thrust his hands into his pockets, hurrying back towards the house. It was difficult to walk with her fine blue dress and her nice shoes, but Beatriz picked up the edge of her skirt and began to run behind him.

"Don't try to come into my room again," she said. "I don't want you to ever come back again."

She tripped and fell, but he did not stop. She lay in the middle of the narrow dirt road. The fine new dress was now smudged and dusty.

X

She sat next to a dry fountain and did not turn when she heard Ramon approaching. But then the great ugly dog appeared at her side, wagging its tail, and she knew it was not Ramon standing behind her.

"Dinner is in an hour," Villanueva said.

"Thank you."

That was all. She did not offer him any polite conversation. Perhaps her silence would inspire him to leave. He stayed, leaning on his cane as the sun set.

She saw then, or perhaps noticed for the first time, a scorpion a few inches from her foot.

"Oh my God," Beatriz said.

He also saw it and, sweeping down, grabbed the scorpion by the tail and held it up.

"Oh my God! Get rid of it!" she yelled.

So he did, tossing it away, and she rushed inside the house. Justiniano joined her at a more leisurely pace.

"How could you do that?" she asked.

"I've been catching scorpions since I was a child. I used to collect them."

"You did?"

"I still have a few specimens lying around."

"That's very ... odd."

"Not in Durango."

"I think it's disgusting," she said.

Justiniano shrugged, and she frowned, biting her lip.

"So how do you grab one without letting it sting you?"

※

She looked at a jar filled with alcohol and tiny baby scorpions floating in it. There was also a wooden frame with several specimens carefully pinned and displayed on black velvet.

"How can you collect them? How can you bear to touch them?"

"You shouldn't be afraid of them. Careful, but not afraid. I had a big black one sting me when I was a boy, but I'm not scared."

"If a scorpion had stung me, I would never get near one again."

"Do you want to hear an interesting story?"

She closed the armoire that contained his specimens and books and sat in one of the rattan chairs across from him. His cane was propped against the wall; the dog lay at his feet.

"A long time ago, a man was taking a stroll when suddenly he saw a white scorpion. He prepared to kill it, but then the scorpion yelled to the man. 'Spare me, spare me,' said the scorpion. 'I must kill you,' said the man. 'Let us make a trade,' cried the scorpion.

"The scorpion asked the man to take him to his home and let him live there upon a cushion of red velvet and feed him insects. If he did this, the scorpion said, he would be very lucky and gain much wealth. So the man did this, and the man became wealthy and well known. The scorpion in turn grew big and fat. He grew so big the man began to distrust it. 'Why, that scorpion is nearly the size of a cat,' the man thought. 'If it ever got angry it could sting me and kill me. Maybe I should kill it first.'

"So the man fed the scorpion its daily ration of insects on a poisoned dish. Immediately the scorpion realized it had been betrayed. 'I am dying, but I will not die alone. You poisoned me, and I shall poison you. Let my poison live in your blood and claim the sons of your body. Let them all live short, painful lives.' And then the scorpion stung the man and died.

"Since then all the sons of the man have died young, but they have been immune to the venom of scorpions because they already carry the venom in their body. That is why I am never afraid of scorpions."

It was getting dark outside, and the library grew thick with shadows. The mechanical bird, sitting on the desk, reflected the sun's dying rays.

Beatriz leaned back.

"You really think I'm going to believe that story?"

"Would you believe when scorpions mate they perform a dance?"

"No," she said, chuckling.

"And sometimes they devour each other."

"As they dance? Why would they do that?" she asked with a smile.

"I suppose it is in their nature."

✕

The days passed and then the weeks. Ramon grew anxious. They had been invited to spend the summer there, and now the summer was coming to an end. Beatriz used to think of Paris often, but now it was a blurry dream, and the thoughts of wealth and marriage had also faded. All that remained around her was the stolid reality of the small house, the fields kissing the orange sky, and Justiniano's slow steps at her side.

"When you are alone, what do you do?" Ramon asked, pacing around the lounge.

Beatriz rode with Justiniano beyond the cemetery, so far that the house disappeared, and farther still with the ugly dog by their side. Afterwards they sat in the library, and she made the mechanical bird play its melodies.

Beatriz shrugged and did not answer.

"Has he touched you?" Ramon asked, his nails running down her left arm.

"He has not."

"He should. If he had you, then maybe he would feel obliged to marry you."

Beatriz shrugged again and caressed the head of the great dog, which sat at her side in the lounge.

"Maybe he does not care for marriage, and it would not matter if you dangled me naked in front of him. Have you thought of that?"

Ramon leaned forward, meaning to strike her. She recoiled. The dog growled, and Ramon stopped, his arm frozen in mid-air. He stepped back, staring at her in silence, and then went towards the door.

"Make it happen," he warned her. "You must make it happen."

✗

Ramon was good with women. He could lie effort-lessly to them. He had swindled half a dozen widows with a few words, a few smiles and his youthful charm. Marriages happened quickly for him. Three, four weeks of courtship and they were before the priest, and just as quickly Ramon and Beatriz had disap-peared, taking with them jewels, money, anything they could.

It was the easiest way to make money, he said. Easier than fake business deals or some of his other shady endeavours.

But what was simple for Ramon became compli-cated for Beatriz. Because she liked Justiniano. Because he was a nice man, open and kind. Unlike them. They were the deceivers, the scorpions lurking between the bed sheets.

So she sat in the library while the mechanical bird sang and Justiniano read his book and her fingers fell upon the chair's arm, marking the melody. She did not dare to speak, afraid some untruths might curl around her tongue; she was of the lineage of betrayers and thieves, both she and Ramon shameless liars since birth.

"Why do you like the bird so much?" he asked.

Sometimes he asked her things like that. Questions springing like water from his mouth. Facts, tidbits of information about scorpions, butterflies, dogs, horses, escaped him all of a sudden, for no reason. He talked suddenly of the animals he adored and then of a story he had heard as a child, turning next to a poem in a book he had been reading.

She did not mind. She'd grown accustomed to this, just as she had grown used to the great dog that always followed him, or that sometimes he had to pause for air when they were walking, like an old man even though he was young.

"It's beautiful," she said.

"I think you should have it," he said.

"It was your mother's."

"Now it is yours."

He looked at her, his face happy and ablaze with a question.

"Thank you," she said.

She felt the lies welling inside her and excused herself before he could speak.

X

The next morning, Justiniano did not come out of his room, and she heard the maids whispering that he was ill again. The doctor arrived.

The house was very quiet. Everybody crept around, talking in low voices, and Beatriz realized as the days bled into one another that they were all awaiting Justiniano's death.

She locked herself in her room. The mechanical bird played its songs. Sitting in the middle of the bed, she could not think, or speak, or move. She only listened to the bird.

Ramon sneaked in late one night and sat next to her.

"It's all ruined," he said. "He'll be dead in a few days. That's what the doctor says."

She did not reply.

"It's your fault. He would have been easy to handle. You mucked it up. Now what'll we do?"

"What we always do," she whispered.

"What *I* always do. You are useless."

He headed towards the vanity and looked at the mechanical bird. The songs had all become the same, and she had not wound it up.

"We'll sell this. And some other things. I've taken a few items. We'll go back to..."

"You can't sell the bird."

"It's got to be worth something."

"But it's mine. He gave it to me."

Ramon turned towards her and slapped her face.

"You'll do as I say."

"No."

"Come here," he said, and pushed her against the bed.

"No," she said.

But she knew this melody. She'd danced this dance before. She did not rouse the house with her screams. This was who they were and what they were, entwined in anger and desperation and pain. *Promenade a deux*. Ramon and Beatriz. This dance had no beginning and no end.

※

She awoke before dawn. The room was dark and quiet. Ramon had left. He always left before morning broke.

Beatriz rose and combed her hair. She dressed slowly, pulling each button with care. She grabbed one of her shoes and looked at it as she did every day. That morning, a blinding white scorpion was nestled in one.

Rather than crushing it, rather than yelling and breaking it into a thousand pieces, she whispered to the scorpion.

"Let us make a trade," she said.

She shook the shoe, and the scorpion fell to the floor. From the floor, it crawled onto her flattened hand. It sat there, as docile as a kitten.

Beatriz went to Ramon's room.

X

The curtains were pulled tight, shielding him from the sun's harsh glare. He lay under the blankets, smelling of salves and sweat.

"It's just a fever," she said.

"Beatriz. My chest hurts."

"Hush."

"I can't get up."

Ramon's skin was waxy, and his lips were chapped as though he had been out in the sun for many hours, but he had spent the whole morning in bed.

"You aren't going to leave me, are you?" he asked, trying to hold her hands. "You're going to sit here and stay with me until I get better."

Beatriz did not reply but only smiled.

"Bita."

He had not called her that in years. Not since she was eight. She remembered a studio, a portrait of the children. While the photographer fiddled with the camera, their father had said they must remain still. She held her breath and clutched Ramon. It seemed to her that, a decade after, she still remained in the same pose, a little girl in her prim dress motionless against a theatrical backdrop.

"Bita, answer me," he demanded, his nails digging into her skin. But the nails were brittle and tore like silk paper.

Beatriz unlaced her hands from his.

⚜

Beatriz changed her clothes for dinner, slipping into a bright yellow gown Ramon had disliked. On the vanity, the mechanical bird sang a tune she had not heard before. As she swept her hair up, she heard a knock at her door.

Justiniano stood there, a flimsy phantom suddenly made solid. He looked tired and his skin was an odd shade, not sickly pale but the smoothness of carved ivory. His eyelashes seemed almost transparent, his eyes drained of colour.

He did not carry his cane. He had moulted, casting off his diseased self.

"How do you feel?" she asked.

"Better," he replied, but there were questions in his eyes.

She touched his face, straightened, and kissed him, brushing away his questions with her hands.

Jaguar Woman

She has forgotten how to be a jaguar but the knowledge sometimes returns in her dreams and she wakes to the dark room and the shape of the man next to her and the distant smell of jungle and night.

Bound inside the stiff dresses, under layers of velvet, ruffs, embroidered roses, it is easy to forget how to shift her shape, how to move sleek and elegant on four legs.

They speak new words to her and the words drive away the words she used to know. They even give her a new name and she watches as her old name is trampled under the hoofs of their horses. The magic is lost.

※

The bearded Spaniard says little to her. He prefers to kiss her and mount her and have her pour his drink for him.

But the priests speak often, furiously. They show her drawings, they explain. The priests have images of martyrs drenched in blood, holding their own heads on a platter, their bodies pierced by arrows.

The priests make her kneel before their blessed Virgin and pray. She has prayed to others before and it is not so difficult to pray to new gods. It is more difficult to have lost her name. Even more difficult to have lost the jaguar shape.

But she does not remember much about those times either. It must have been years ago. She's been the Spaniard's mistress for an eternity. It has been like this forever, eating at his table, sleeping in his bed. Although it must not have been forever; she remembers there was a time when she could barely understand him and now his words are clearer although his meaning is the same.

Around the city she looks for other jaguars. The familiar faces have vanished. Perhaps she imagined it all.

In dreams her lord-father's white house is bright and real. She walks through that house and watches the jaguars laying on the floor, their yellow eyes smiling. The youngest daughter of the Abode of Jaguars sits with her brothers, their tails twitching and their fur shimmering.

Her brothers have been skinned.

Her white house was razed.

She is a jaguar no longer.

X

The Spaniard brings her trinkets. She would like to push them aside, but playful cat that she was and still sometimes is, she tiptoes around the table, watches the objects. When she was a jaguar she ran through the jungle without a single sound disturbing the singing birds and the frogs, the snakes and the *caiman*. She would hunt the tapir, her teeth piercing its skull.

His latest offering is a hand mirror. It shines blindingly under the sun and then she turns it and observes her eyes.

They are dark. They are pretty. But they are not jaguar eyes.

She sobs and he does not understand. He thought it would make her happy. His fingers disentangle themselves from her hair, pulling away brusquely and he's gone.

Their bedroom is small and it is stuffed with all his things. His clothes, even his furniture intimidates ... his smell lingers. He's forced his whole world into the tiny room and she must stand with her back pressed against the wall, without enough space to take more than two steps, tiptoeing around the objects he loves.

There's so much of him in the room, in the house, that even when he's not there he's still near, fingers gripping her arms, mouth against her mouth.

He's caged her.

That night she tries to sleep at the very edge of the bed but he pulls her towards him, locked in a firm embrace. He will not let her go.

He will never let her go.

X

Yesterday she smashed the mirror. When it shattered the mirror laughed and she laughed with it.

There was a woman in the mirror but it was not her. She remembers her face differently. It was a face with strong jaws, sharp teeth, yellow eyes.

The woman in the mirror would not be able to climb up a tree or let out a fierce growl.

She tells him the mirror broke, an accident. He says he'll buy her a new one.

She doesn't want another mirror but he insists and she must accept in the way she must accept all things from him. There is no room for discussion. He speaks kindly, almost lovingly, but he jams words down her ears, sneaks fingers under her skirts, demands in whispers.

She cannot ask. She cannot plead. There is nothing left to barter with.

X

She forgot how to be a jaguar but the knowledge sometimes returns in her dreams.

Today she opened her eyes and felt the jaguar shifting inside her skull.

In the dark she can feel the jaguar clawing at her and wanting to tear its way out through that delicate human skin. She bites her lip and draws blood. She scratches her belly, her nails tracing chaotic patterns of lines and swirls.

It stops suddenly, pulling back like the tide.

She is back in the bed, with the man next to her and the smell of wax and leather overtakes her. The jungle is gone.

But now her eyes glint in the dark and she knows.

X

Tomorrow she will cast aside that wretched human body. Tomorrow she will regain the jaguar's shape.

Tomorrow she will pounce upon her sleeping lover. She will choke his screams with her weight. She will bite into his neck and chest. Her teeth will pierce through flesh and bones. She will tear chunks of meat and watch as his blood spills onto the bed, then drips gently down to the floor until it becomes a lake and it swallows the whole room.

She will swim in that lake just as she swam in the waterhole under the shade of the trees.

Tomorrow she is a jaguar again.

Nahuales

The *nahual* smiles, showing off its yellowed teeth, as it stands under the streetlamp. He wears a black leather jacket, smokes cheap cigarettes, but he is still a *nahual*. There is the whiff of mountains about him and the glint of the coyote in his eyes. I've never seen a *nahual*, but I heard of them through my great-grandmother. Old-lady stories. Folktales. The tales steer me to the other side of the street, avoiding him. He notices, the corner of his mouth twitches, but I head down the steps towards the subway.

Safe, sitting inside the orange subway car, the smell of the mountains and the *matorral* fades and I am once more in Mexico City. A boy walks down the aisle selling bubble gum. A teenager bobs his head up and down to the music from his headphones. A man reads a newspaper. Once more *nahuales* are stories, very old stories, and nothing more.

And yet I place three nails in my bag the next morning.

ᚷ

Three days later I step out and feel the city changing. The scent of pines and shrubs where there ought to be only smog.

I look at the homeless man sprawled in an alley and wonder if his grey shape betrays another nature.

I take the underpass to the subway, quickening my pace. When I emerge, I almost bump into him.

The *nahual* from the other night with his black jacket. He's with two others this time. They're also dressed in leather; they also smoke cheap cigarettes that stain the fingers.

The one in black smiles at me and he says something I can't make out. Maybe he's trying to put a spell on me.

I can deal with this.

I duck my head and toss the nails behind me, and they do not follow.

I turn to look at them as I reach the steps. They're laughing. It resembles the barking of wild dogs.

※

I place the rosemary and the knitting needles under my bed for protection. I carry nails to ward my tracks. But that doesn't make them go away. They remain there, waiting by the subway station.

In my great-grandmother's time, in her hometown, they tied a poor, bawling goat to a post to lure the *nahual*, then dropped a crucifix at its feet when it appeared. My great-grandmother shot the *nahual* in the head herself. It had killed her sister. The only thing she regretted was the bawling of the goat as the *nahual* tore its belly open.

It is impossible to attempt that these days. Where would one get a goat? How could one fire a rifle? The only rifles I've seen are in the sepia-coloured pictures of my great-grandmother's youth, she with the weapon against her shoulder, staring squarely at the camera, the corpse of the *nahual* at her feet. A dark mountain range behind. A land of forests and monsters.

I lower my head, I try to hide between the folds of my clothing and walk faster. Faster, faster. The click of my shoes against the cement. Their shadows behind me until I slip into the subway car. Until it pulls from the station and I can breathe again.

⚶

The walk from work to the subway has become unbearable. Each night they are there. Sometimes they sit, hunched down, drinking from green bottles. Other times they lean against the wall, arms crossed. But they're always there.

The nails will only do so much and I fear my method of protection might be losing its strength. Meanwhile, their grins seem to grow wider. I can almost hear the snapping of their jaws as I rush forward, trying to move as quickly as my heels will allow.

I never understand what they say to me. I don't want to understand. Garbled nonsense which might be a threat. Or an entreaty.

I take a taxi one Friday, unable to face the walk to the subway. But I can't afford one each night. Only the subway can take me to my apartment.

X

The *nahuales*, not content with inhabiting the outskirts of the station, have made the neighbourhood their home. Shadows and cracks appear where they have never been before, and the buildings resemble mountains. One day I fear I shall walk out the door and find myself deep in the *matorral*, the dense thickets making it impossible to make my way back.

X

Fear has made me look for different routes. But eventually, just like all rivers lead to the sea, I must make my way into the station. And they'll be there. It does not matter if I approach it from the north or the south, if I take the underpass, or round the streets. They find me.

They have grown brazen in their approach. No longer content to whisper and watch me, they sniff and touch a strand of hair as I walk by. Sneak a hand up my arm.

They are so close I think I see the ticks in their matted hair, which is like fur. Their eyes are narrow, opportunistic.

Their voices, as I descend into the station, bounce off the walls with vicious glee.

※

The rain comes and seems to flush the *nahuales* away. Once again I can walk to the station, heels splashing in the puddles.

I am relieved.

But then I spot it, gnawing at garbage: a great black dog. It growls at me. Two other dogs appear and join the black one.

I take a step back.

It takes a step forward.

I run, back through the underpass, back to the street. I take off my heels and run barefoot, nylons tearing and sweat dripping down my neck.

The pack chases me across a forest of tall pines. I wade through a stream and emerge on the other bank, until I reach the safety of a café and rush inside. I look out the window and see the dogs' eyes in the dark. They glow yellow, like the stub of a cigarette.

I hear laughter and three men walk from the shadows. The one in the black jacket opens his mouth and smoke curls out of it, like incense rising in the night. He smiles at me.

⚹

I wait for an hour before I leave the café, but I do not seed my tracks with nails.

When I get home, I climb into bed without taking my clothes off and press my bag against my chest. I think of the goat tied and bawling in the dark.

The moon shines yellow and round through the curtains. The din of traffic grows distant and the night is blacker than ink, all the city lights blotted out.

The door creaks open as a black dog nuzzles his way into my bedroom. Two other dogs pad behind him.

The black dog sniffs and approaches my bed. Its bark is close to laughter.

I draw the sharp knitting needle from my bag and grin before plunging it into his neck.

THE DOPPELGÄNGERS

The longest we lived in one place was seven months.

My parents suffered from wanderlust. I didn't know there was a term for their condition until I was ten and I found the word in a dictionary. It kind of made sense that they'd be under the thrall of some weird German and hard-to-pronounce disease, seeing as my dad was an intellectual snob and suffering from run-of-the-mill idiocy would be a bit too ignoble to bear.

Later on I met the doppelgängers and that explained even more. Or maybe it didn't. Who knows.

✕

It started with the Mexican debt crisis of 1982. One day we had a house and one day we didn't. Oddly enough, I don't think my parents minded that much. Something in them had been itching to roll out maps, set forth and conquer new territory.

We packed the cactus, the books and a couple of suitcases and headed away.

For the first few years it was fun. We went down to the coast and I got to start a seashell collection. My mother braided my hair as we rode the car and the radio blared the songs they liked and my parents sang to them. Then we moved further south and it was warmer and we lazily slipped into the Yucatan peninsula. But by the time we were heading out of Veracruz I was fed up with the constant shuffle.

The apartments we took were bare of almost any furniture because we wouldn't be there long enough to accumulate possessions. We didn't even unpack much of our stuff anymore. And though they said it would be different this time around, this time we'd settle and plant some roots, that it would all be better soon, I knew my parents were liars.

I didn't even have the cactus – it had rotted away from overwatering.

I think it might have been my anger which brought the doppelgängers but I can't really say. They were there one day, like mushrooms sprouting after the rain and boy, was that a rainy September. Mexico City should have been exciting but with my soggy socks and the second-hand uniform I had to wear to school, all the excitement died away.

It was a private school. Catholic. But my aunt insisted on it and she was, after all, paying for my education, though her generosity did not extend to a new uniform.

Things had gone worse than expected in Jalapa. Short of cash, my parents turned to my dad's sister for assistance. Aunt Carolina had money to spare, but would not part with it without making some explicit demands. That included a proper Catholic school for me.

My dad was a journalist and a bibliophile. My mother a photographer. I still have some of her photographs from back then. Black-and-white images which show the long, empty stretches of highway, the changing Mexican landscape.

My dad went to work for a small printer of schoolbooks. My mother went to work part-time as a cashier.

My mother was supposed to pick me up after school, but she was often tardy. She had an innate inability to tell time and seemed to function on an entirely different schedule than the rest of the world. Active at three a.m., out of bed by noon. This had not been much of an issue before, but now, with my dad employed full-time and my mother with her part-time job – they had been freelancers before – she had to pick me up and she was late.

The nuns at school, who had the gentle touch of scorpions, glared at her, white teeth bared, whenever she appeared, heels clicking.

It didn't matter how much I begged her to be on time, she never listened.

One afternoon, as I waited after school, long after the rest of my classmates, I saw my mother and father across the street. They were holding a large umbrella. I thought it was odd that they'd both come for me.

A few minutes later my mother arrived. She was all wet. She didn't have an umbrella and was cursing – she cursed often and loudly – about her employer, that bitch who snapped her fingers at her.

I asked her what had happened to her umbrella and she said she'd lost it two days ago.

We got into the beat-up car that was a source of shame to me. Everyone else had a fancier vehicle. I pressed my face against the window and looked out at the shiny, new cars going by and I wished we could go to Acapulco. We never vacationed. There was no money for such frivolities and anyway, my father liked to remind us, Acapulco was for the bourgeois.

✕

We lived in Aunt Carolina's house, a large, old structure wallpapered in different shades of yellow. It was a very dignified home. Aunt Carolina echoed it in her prim dresses with flower patterns and her sensible shoes. My mother, who'd fallen in love in university and subsequently dropped out and married my father, seemed to be removed an entire generation from Carolina even though they were close in age.

My mother was pretty and bubbly. She liked to dress in tight jeans and tighter shirts, take photographs, and spend plenty of time going out at nights. My aunt did not approve of this, especially the going out at night because my father had a job to attend to and they couldn't very well take off as they did before, could they?

My father agreed and nodded and said his sister was a smart woman, but he still found way too many excuses to drink and when aunt Carolina wasn't looking he'd slip into his favourite leather jacket and trot off to read at the park or play pool and smoke cigarettes. Talking about Camus never made anyone a single peso, and the result was any extra money we had went towards books, drinks and smokes.

My father took me with him to the pool hall sometimes. I was only a kid, but there were plenty of youths there anyway and nobody enforced the sign that said "minors will not be allowed in the premises."

He liked to talk philosophy and literature while he played with Seferino, a high school teacher with a high-pitched voice, and Tomas, a translator of French novels.

I'd listen to them, never understanding a word, and drank lots of lime sodas until it was time to go back to the house. Other kids at my school could say their dad had taken them horseback riding or bought them a new toy during the weekend, but all I could claim was a couple of lime sodas and his back turned to me while he shot an eight ball.

One evening when we were heading home – my father was talking about the book he'd read the day before, his words slightly slurred – I caught sight of a man who looked exactly like him walking on the opposite side of the street. The man was wearing a very nice suit and shiny shoes and his hair was slicked back, cut short instead of tied in a ponytail. He carried a briefcase.

I tugged at my father's arm, trying to make him look, but he didn't and then the man turned the corner.

My dad laughed with his deep, vibrant voice and he said he had a few pesos and we could stop to buy a hot plantain from the street seller pushing his little cart.

X

They had a *kermesse* at school and all the mothers made treats, cooked tamales and prepared *orchata* water. Not my mother. She could mix all the right chemicals to develop negatives but she couldn't – or wouldn't – produce a platter of *tostadas*. The result was that I was the only kid at school that didn't bring any food. To top it off, my mother had braided my hair and I didn't like it anymore because the other kids said I looked like an Indian, like the maid's kid.

I stared at the colourful stands with their signs made on pieces of cardboard and their paper flowers.

I stared at the mothers behind the stands and their children.

I saw my mother's double by a food stand wearing a conservative beige blouse and small earrings, very much unlike my real mother with her tight shirts, the loud laughter, the cheap jewellery she liked to wear, the camera resting on her hip.

The double stared at me.

X

My mother worked in a shop in the Zona Rosa – formerly an area of upscale boutiques, most of its cachet now lost – which was the worst possible location for a woman of her temperament, especially due to the strategic positioning of a camera store with all sorts of fancy filters, tripods and lenses.

One afternoon, when we stopped by to pick up her paycheck, she ended up spending almost the whole of it on some camera equipment that took her fancy. When we stepped out I saw a copy of my mother ride off in a taxi, her long hair cut short, and sporting some pearls I'd never seen her wear.

That night my mother and father had a row over the camera equipment.

It was like this with them frequently. They'd yell, insult, even come to blows – if this was the case, I had to stop them – and then make up in a couple of days.

I hated it and I hated them.

I pressed a pillow over my head until I heard a door slam shut. After a little while I stepped out towards the window, staring at the moon and wondering if all the other kids had to deal with clowns like these.

Then I looked down onto the street and saw a man and a woman staring up at me. I placed my hand against the glass, as if greeting them, but then grew afraid and returned to bed.

X

The bitter rain continued to fall, clogging sewers and causing floods, threatening to return Mexico City to the swamp from which it had risen.

The nuns' lessons were stale and my mind wandered when they spoke. Because it rained so much we couldn't have recess in the little courtyard. We ate our lunch at our desks and were supposed to read quietly instead of playing games.

I read a thick dictionary. I loved learning the meaning of words. That's how I had come upon wanderlust and many other interesting definitions. My father, himself a lover of words, gave me a piece of bubble gum for every difficult word I acquired.

That day, as the rain sang its litany, I found a new word. It was chance. My hands opening the dictionary to a random page, a finger falling upon the letters. Doppelgänger. An evil double. An alter ego.

I looked across the street that afternoon – my mother was late, again – and saw a man and a woman with my parents' faces. They nodded at me. I nodded in return.

X

Aunt Carolina had dinner parties twice a month. She ordered tiny little breads and salty crackers from the nearby bakery, and cousins and friends I had never met descended upon the house. The men all wore suits and ties and were all *licenciado* something, all slightly pudgy and greyed, unlike my father, who stood quiet, thin and swathed in his leather jacket.

The women wore dresses similar to my aunt's, sensible shoes and painted smiles. None of them understood my mother's interest in installing a darkroom in the house – we'd always had one before – nor her open laughter.

These people's children were chubby, unruly, regular kids who got to visit Acapulco. We were too good for Acapulco, for these reunions, for the whole freaking world.

The parties left my parents looking slightly frayed. They fought after them. Late at night my mother accused my father of having dragged her to Mexico

City, of living like beggars. He accused her of ingratitude, of spending too much money and wearing flashy clothes and flirting loudly with everyone they bumped into.

After one memorable fight my mother took the car, threatening to drive off and never come back, succeeding only in crashing the old thing.

In the morning my mother was tight-lipped. We boarded the bus. All the windows were misty and you couldn't see outside. The bus was packed with people in their suits, carrying briefcases, looking straight ahead.

My mother found us a seat and we spent the ride in silence. I rubbed away the mist veiling the outside with the palm of my hand, but all I saw was greyness and rain.

X

My father lost his job at the beginning of December.

This made Aunt Carolina angry and my mother even angrier. She had been planning to quit her own job and try to do some freelancing again. My father's sudden unemployment meant she'd have to stay.

My father said if she wanted to split she could do it and she said she wouldn't leave me with him, an irresponsible drunkard who couldn't even ride the subway three stops up the street and push paper clips around a desk.

My father countered with my mother's lack of punctuality and her unnecessary displays of bare flesh, as though she were still sixteen when she had passed thirty.

Banging of doors, drawers empty, suitcases filled with clothes and then emptied as the inevitable making up took place.

But unlike other times it felt like they had reached a boiling point and there were fights every third day, and with the *posadas* in full swing my father was drinking more, my mother was screaming louder and I was learning more words than I had ever learned before, just trying to bury my head in the dictionary or melt into the wallpaper.

On December 23 they came to blows. My mother flung a vase towards my father. It hit him smack in the face. He responded by rolling up a newspaper and hitting her on the back.

"Will you stop!" I yelled, which was what I usually yelled.

And they did, looking contrite.

And then, after they had cooled down, my mother came looking for me and said "Sweetheart, it'll all be better soon," and she asked if I wanted my hair braided.

Only it was never better. That's what they promised as we skipped from town to town, as we drove down the highway with the windows rolled down, as the years melted.

It'll be better soon. My parents were liars of the worst sort.

I lay with my hands pressed against my belly, feeling a knot in my gut. Everything was quiet. I listened to my own breathing.

Without turning on the lights I tiptoed to the front of the house and opened the door.

The doubles were waiting patiently, sitting on the steps. They walked in and went up the stairs, towards my parent's room. I went back to bed.

※

Three weeks later my mother sold all her photo equipment and asked for a full-time position at the shop. My father, sobered up, with his hair cut and in a suit, looked much more respectable and landed a job at a paper factory writing neat productivity reports.

They didn't smile, but they didn't fight either.

In July they bought a new car. We decided to drive it to Acapulco for the weekend.

As my father was swinging the suitcase inside I chanced to look behind and saw a man and a woman by the curb, looking very much like my parents. He wore a leather jacket, she had a camera strapped around her neck.

They raised their heads, as if to signal me.

Driving with Aliens in Tijuana

I sit behind the counter and hum a bolero. Humans come in and out of the gift shop. Aliens pause to look at plastic cacti and cheap maracas.

A young guy stops in front me. The man isn't very touristy. He's wearing a black suit and a tie. Hair slicked back. Sunglasses. He's with an alien resembling a large octopus.

"My friend likes your voice," the man says.

"Thanks," I say.

"Would you like to make a lot of money?"

I raise my eyebrows high.

"His species has a peculiar method of vocalization and a complex language system," the young man says quickly. "Human voices and speech interest them. A lot. We're spending the week in Tijuana and he wants you to hang out with us."

"You're kidding, right?" I ask.

Despite living in Mexico's only Authorized Intergalactic Zone and the brochures with nice, smiling blond people hugging an alien sitting on the rack up front, I've never heard such a request before. I've never even seen an extraterrestrial from the other side of the counter. They come in, pay, leave. I stay, restock the maracas, flip through magazines.

A guy once walked into the store and he had a shirt that said "Schrödinger's cat is not dead" and I asked him what that meant. He said it was a paradox and explained the cat was dead and was not dead at the same time.

Some days I feel I'm the cat and I'm not sure if I've been gassed with poison.

"Nope," he says and slides a prepaid credit card towards me. "Check the balance."

The sun blazes outside, incessant. The radio sings about September. The old fan is whirring behind me.

I stare at the man and the alien and I'm wondering if I'm currently dead-alive or alive-dead.

※

I've never been in a black sports car. Much less a sports car with an alien in the backseat. I look out the window and hum as we drive up a hill, away from downtown.

There's an illusory calmness about the city when you watch it from afar. You can't see the drunk crowds moving through Avenida Revolucion. You can't hear the men whistling at the girls in miniskirts. You can't spot the sixteen corpses with plastic bags around their heads laying on the side of the road. Tijuana is a city of drugs, crimes and whores. Of factories churning out cheap merchandise for off-world export, and the even cheaper workers locked inside.

You can't see that at night. From afar, there's only the city lights and the slopes of the land.

"How long you been working for it?" I ask Rollo when we have a brief pause and the alien lets us turn off the stereo we've been blasting all day long.

"Two years," he says.

"Do you spend all your time translating?"

"No. Some of this, some of that.   I'm his boy Friday. I run errands. I get lunch."

"What does it eat?"

"Kittens," he says very seriously.

I give him a horrified look and Rollo cracks a smile. He chuckles.

"You believed me," he says, fingers tapping the steering wheel.

Traffic is very slow in Tijuana. The alien doesn't want to walk so we inch forward. It's alright. I'm kinda enjoying myself.

"What should I know?" I say. "I'm not even sure what species he is."

Rollo makes this weird sound that's like "kotch'o." I try to repeat it, but I can't say it. The alien in the back-seat laughs.

At least, I think it laughs. It ripples and snorts, tentacles quivering slightly.

The alien repeats the sound Rollo made. Kotch'o.

I try again. Fail miserably. They both laugh some more.

The alien tries to teach me a simple phrase. Kikawi kotch'o. I try it again and I do alright.

Rollo smiles. I think the alien smiles too.

※

The alien likes to drink and go to nightclubs. We stop at a karaoke bar around three a.m. and I sing four songs in a row.

They don't have boleros. It's a pity. I make do with 1980s pop music.

The alien twitches its tentacles and nods at me. I'm getting to know it better and I think I'm understanding its non-verbal cues now. Slow blinks. Fast blinks. Low growls. Tentacles still or agitated.

The alien's colour has changed from purple to a shade of blue that's like a perfect sky; the sky of the desert, far from the city limits.

"It's the booze," Rollo explains when I sit down next to them and someone else grabs the microphone. "The equivalent to our blushing mechanism. He's too warm."

"Is it dangerous?"

"It's alright," Rollo says. He orders a bucket full of ice cubes and when they bring it to our table the alien rolls the tips of his tentacles in it.

The alien isn't thrilled with sake, so we end up leaving not long after that. Rollo drops me off at my place and they drive back to their hotel.

)(

In the three days we've been hanging out I haven't seen Rollo wear anything except perfectly tailored black suits. Today's jacket has an almost imperceptible grey pinstripe. He's got another rental car. It's white.

"Hey, you ready?" he asks.

I feel my aunt's eyes burrowing into my back from our apartment window. She doesn't like this arrangement. Last night, after the karaoke, she yelled at me.

But it's a lot of money.

I'm itching to get away from home and nod curtly, slamming the door. I look towards the backseat.

"Where's your buddy?" I ask.

"He's got a hangover," Rollo says.

"I didn't know aliens could get hangovers."

"Well, something like that. He wants to hit the opera tonight. Last time we were on Earth we went to the Met."

"I've never been to the opera," I say.

Once I heard a group of Russians singing at a café. I'm not sure what they were singing. It wasn't boleros and it wasn't in Spanish. I don't know what the Met is and before I met Rollo I didn't know the right way to say *après-midi*. Hell, I didn't even know what that meant, but Rollo says lots of fancy words. He rolls with Italian and German, and then he shrugs and says *dela vkusa* and *J' ai oublié*, and I ain't got much of an idea of what it's all about. It's very cool.

"He's crazy about it," Rollo says. "We're going to buy you a dress for tonight."

"What, you kidding?"

"Nope."

"That's super," I say.

I feel a little ashamed walking into a nice store in jeans and a T-shirt. Rollo seems to be in his element. He orders the employees around and demands to see several black dresses.

"Why black?" I ask.

"He can't see colour," Rollo says.

"Dogs can't see colour either."

Rollo gives me a weird look. I'm ashamed of having said that. I've compared his employer to a pet. Even though he looks a bit like an octopus, he ain't one.

"What's his planet like?" I ask, trying to change the subject.

"Cold."

"It must live in an aquatic city with glass bubble-domes," I say.

Rollo smiles. "Now why would you say that?"

I saw a drawing of something like that. Atlantis, it was called. I shrug.

"His planet is cold. But we live on the third moon of Ishvera. It's a bit warm there. He's got most of his business in Ishvera."

"What kind of business?"

"Import and export," Rollo says and he presses a pair of black high heels into my hands. "Try these on."

I get to wear my hair up that night. I've never worn my hair up before, not even for my *quinceañera* party. My aunt said it cost too much to rent the salon, so I ended up having cake and soda at my apartment.

I get to eat caviar and drink wine. I arrive home at four in the morning, singing so loud I wake up all my cousins.

✗

I've picked up a Kotchei-Spanish dictionary and I try to find the phrase for "good morning." The alien looks very pleased when I try to say it and I'm beaming as Rollo hands me a glass of tomato juice.

It's the first time I've been in their hotel room. It's huge. The living room is twice the size of our apartment and there's a piano by the window.

The view from the balcony is still a shitty grey sky with shitty grey buildings, factories left and right. Not as bad as Mexico City, but then nothing is as bad as Mexico City. They say Tijuana is the country's Authorized Intergalactic Zone because Mexico City was so polluted the aliens dropped dead when they landed there.

"We've got to get some of that coloured marijuana," Rollo tells me as we sit out in the balcony.

"What, to smoke it?"

"To drink it. We'll make a tincture out of it."

"Oh," I say. "He can't smoke?"

"Nah."

I drink my juice and nod.

If you squint your eyes, from the balcony's angle, Tijuana doesn't seem that bad. A gazillion times worse than Ishvera – I've been looking at pictures of it – but not puke awful.

Rollo must be thinking the same thing I'm thinking 'cause he turns towards me and smiles.

"He's considering taking you with us."

"What? Seriously?" I ask, almost spilling my juice over my lap.

"Yes. He loves your voice. He thinks you're aesthetically pleasing."

"What? No. I must be butt-ugly to them."

"The exotic factor. All that hair and the big eyes."

Hair is all I've ever had. Black, thick and long. I'm no beauty queen. Perhaps that doesn't matter to the squids.

"You're not hairy," I say.

"How do you know?"

I elbow him. We laugh. Rollo teaches me Kotchei words. I can't remember half of them by the time I get home. My aunt yells. I slam the bathroom door shut and sit on the toilet, staring at the wall.

※

We spend the next day listening to opera in the alien's hotel room. It's incredibly loud. Rollo explains what each piece is about, the name of the composer. At least, he does for a while. It's hours and hours of singing, so eventually he stops.

Room service brings a mountain of food. We drink *mezcal*. We switch from opera to punk. I fall asleep.

I wake up after midnight and the living room is quiet. The couch is comfy but my aunt will kill me if I don't get home before dawn. I'm guessing Rollo's asleep and I feel bad waking him, but I need a ride home.

I stumble towards Rollo's room and slide the door open.

He's not asleep.

At first I'm not sure what I'm seeing. Tentacles and limbs in a bizarre arrangement. My slow brain eventually catches on to the fact that the alien is fucking Rollo. It's like a bad horror movie. Like the reverse from those magazine covers that had them green Venusian girls fucked by Earth's astronauts.

The alien turns its head to stare at me with its great double pupils.

I walk back to the living room.

※

In the morning Rollo takes me home. It's a silver car. The white one's gone.

Rollo's quiet. We stop at an intersection and I turn to look at him. He tilts his head to the side and glances at me with a silent question mark hanging over his head.

I want to ask him if it hurts. I want to ask him if he hates it. I want to ask him if he likes it. I want to ask him if he misses other humans when he's sitting on that third moon. I want to ask him if it's humiliating. I want to ask him if he's happy.

I want to ask him if it doesn't matter because we're in Tijuana and we're all getting fucked.

I want to ask if we're dead-alive, like the cat who got gassed. Or if it's alive-dead.

I want to ask him.

The light changes to green.

I never ask him.

FLASH FRAME

The sound is yellow.

X

It was when you could still make a living freelancing in Mexico City. Nowadays, it's wire services and regurgitated shit, but in 1982 rags still needed original content. I did a couple of funky articles, the latest about the cheapest whore in the city for *Enigma!*, a mixed bag of crime stories, tits and freakish news items. It paid well and on time.

I also did articles for an arts and culture magazine which, I was hoping, would turn into a permanent position. But when it came time to gather rent money, *Enigma!* was first on my mind.

The trouble was that there was a new assistant editor at *Enigma!* and he didn't like the old crop of stringers. To get past him, I had to pitch harder. I needed better stories. Stories he couldn't refuse.

The crime stuff was a bust, nothing good recently, so I moved onto sex and decided to swing by El Tabu, a porno cinema housed in a great, art deco building. It's gone now, bulldozed to make way for condos.

Back then, it still stood, both ruined and glorious. The great days of porno of the 70s had come and gone, and videocassettes were invading the market. El Tabu stood defiant, yet crumbling. Inside you could find rats as big as rabbits, statues holding torchlights in their hands and a Venus in the lobby. Elegant, ancient and large. Some people came to sleep during a double feature and used the washrooms to take a bath. Others came for the shows. Some were peddling. I'm not going to explain what they were peddling; you figure it out.

It was a good place to listen to chatter. A stringer needs that chatter. One afternoon, I gathered my notebook and my tape recorder, paid for a ticket and went looking for Sebastian, the projectionist, who had a knack for gossiping and profiting from it.

Sebastian hadn't heard any interesting things – there was some vague stuff about a whole squadron of Russian prostitutes in a high-rise apartment building near downtown and university students selling themselves for sex, but I'd heard it before. Then Sebastian got a funny look on his face and asked me for a cigarette. This meant he was zeroing in on the good stuff.

"I don't think I should tell you, but there's a religious group coming in every Thursday," he said, as he took a puff. "Order of something. Have you heard of Enrique Zozoya?"

"No," I said.

"He's the one renting the place. For the group."

"A porno theatre doesn't seem like the nicest place for a congregation."

"I think it's some sort of sex cult. I can't tell because I don't look. They bring their own projectionist and I have to wait in the lobby," Sebastian explained.

"So how do you know it's a sex cult and they're not worshipping Jesus?"

"I can't watch, but I can very well hear some stuff. It doesn't sound like Jesus."

✕

There was no Wikipedia. You couldn't Google a name. What you could do was go through archives and dig out microfiches. Fortunately, Enrique Zozoya wasn't that hard to find. An ex-hippie activist in the 60s, he had turned New Age guru in the early 70s, doing horoscopes. He'd peaked mid-decade, selling natal charts to a few celebrities, then sinking into anonymity. There was nothing about him in the past few years, but he'd obviously found a new source of employment in this religious order.

Armed with the background I had clubbed together, I ventured to El Tabu the following Thursday with my worn backpack containing my notebook, my tape recorder and my cigarettes. The tape recorder was a bit banged up and sometimes it wouldn't play right, or it would switch on record for no reason, but I didn't have money to get a new one. The cigarettes, on the other hand, could be counted upon on any occasion.

Sebastian didn't look too happy to see me, but I mentioned some money and he softened. He agreed to sneak me into the theatre before the show started, onto the second balcony where I would not be spotted. The place was huge and the crowd that gathered every Thursday was small. They wouldn't notice me.

Sitting behind a red velvet curtain, eating pistachios, I waited for the show to start. At around eight o'clock about fifty people walked in. I peeked from behind my hiding place and recognized Enrique Zozoya as he moved to the front of the theatre. He was dressed in a bright yellow outfit. He said a few words which I couldn't make out and then he sat down.

That was that. The projection started.

It was a faux-Roman movie. Rome as seen by some Hollywood producer. It could have been filmed in 1954 and directed by DeMille. Except DeMille wouldn't have featured bare tits. Lots of women, half-dressed, in what was some sort of throne room. In the background I noticed several men and women, less comely and muscled. Slightly unsettling in their looks. There was something twisted and perverted about them. But the camera focused on the people in the foreground, the young and beautiful women giggling and feeding grapes to a guy. There were men, chests bared, leaning against a column. The tableau was completed by an actor who was playing an emperor and his companion, a dark-haired beauty.

It lasted about ten minutes. Just before the lights whet on, I caught sight of a flash frame. A single, brief image of a woman in a yellow dress.

That was it. Enrique Zozoya stood to speak to the audience. I didn't hear what he was saying – I was sitting too far back – but it wasn't anything of consequence because just a short while later everyone was out the door.

I left feeling dejected. There was nothing to write about. Ten minutes of some porno, probably imported from Italy. And even that had been disappointing. You could hardly see much of anything in that scene they'd chosen; bare breasts, yes, but nothing more.

What a waste.

X

I returned the following Thursday because I kept thinking there had to be something more. Maybe the previous show had been a bust, but this one might be better.

Sebastian let me in after I shared my cigarettes and I sat down in the balcony. People arrived, took their seats, Enrique Zozoya in his yellow outfit said a few words and the projection began. It was the same deal, only this time the group was larger. Maybe a hundred people.

I was disappointed to see the film was the one we had watched last time. Not the same section, but it was obviously the same movie. This time, the sequence took place in a Roman circus where aristocrats had gathered to watch a chariot race. There was more nudity and the erotic content had been amped a bit, with a stony-looking emperor sitting with two naked girls in his lap – one of them the dark-haired woman from the previous sequence – fondling their breasts. Unfortunately, he seemed more interested in the race than the women.

The music was loud and of poor quality. There was no dialogue. There hadn't been any dialogue in the previous scene either, which struck me as a bit odd, since you'd expect a few jokes or poor attempts at breathless sexiness at this point.

The emperor mouthed a few words and I realized the audio track must have been removed. The music playing was probably layered onto the film to replace the original soundtrack and had nothing to do with the film. Someone had taken the added effort of inserting moans and sighs into the audio track, but the dialogue track had clearly been lost. Not that it would be much of a loss for this type of flick.

The emperor mouthed something else and again I noticed a flash frame – a few seconds long – of a woman in a yellow dress. She was sitting in a throne room, held a fan against her face, and her blond hair was laced with jewels.

The film was cut off shortly afterwards and the audience left.

I drummed my fingers against my steno pad. What I had was nothing but some European exploitation movie, probably filmed in the late 70s by the looks of it, which for some odd reason attracted a group of about a hundred people to its weekly screening. And it wasn't even screened completely, just a few minutes of it.

Why?

X

I visited the Cineteca Nacional on Monday, which was the place to find information about movies. I had very little to go by, and looking through newspaper clips and data sheets proved fruitless. I asked one of the employees at the Cineteca's Documentation and Information Centre for assistance, and she said she'd phone me if she found something.

I decided to move in a different direction, expanding my knowledge of Zozoya. He'd been a film student before turning to astrology, even shooting a couple of shorts. Aside from that, which might explain how he got hold of this bit of film, there was nothing new.

Tuesday I pounded some copy for the arts and culture magazine, ready to give up on El Tabu.

Wednesday I had a nightmare.

I lay in bed when a woman crawled up, onto me.
She was naked, but wore a golden headpiece with a
veil. Her skin was a sickly yellow, as though she were
jaundiced.

She pressed her breasts against my chest and began
rubbing herself against me. I touched her hips, but
withdrew my hand, quickly. There was something
unpleasant about the texture of her skin.

I lifted a hand, pulling at her veil.

But she had no face. It was only a yellow blur.

When I woke up, it was nearly nine and I was late
for my meeting with the editor of the arts and culture
magazine. I turned in my copy and left quickly. I didn't
feel well. I went home, laid down, and spent most of
the day dozing in front of the television set. I looked at
my steno pad and the lined, yellow pages reminded me
of leprous skin. I didn't do much writing that afternoon.

Thursday evening I returned to El Tabu.

Journalists know when they've caught the scent of a
good story. It's a sixth sense, learning to distinguish the
golden nuggets amongst the pebbles. I knew I had a
nugget. I just couldn't see it yet.

This time the sequence took place in a banquet
hall, with all the guests wearing masks and sitting

naked. Several of the actors were unsuitable for such a scene, with obvious physical flaws, including scars. A few of them looked filthy, as though they had not bathed in several weeks. The emperor and the dark-haired woman next to him were the only ones not wearing masks. They both stared rigidly ahead, as the guests began to copulate on the floor.

The woman whispered something to the emperor. He nodded.

This time it was not a flash frame. We were treated to a full minute of footage showing the woman in the yellow dress, the fan held in front of her face, yellow curtains billowing behind her and allowing us a glimpse of a long hallway full of pillars. The woman crooked a finger towards the audience, as if calling for us.

The film switched back to the banquet scene where the young woman sitting next to the emperor had collapsed. Slaves were trying to revive her, but her tongue poked out of her mouth grotesquely. The soundtrack, with its moans and sighs, was completely unsuited for this scene.

The lights went on. I listened carefully, trying to catch what Zozoya said. It sounded like he was chanting. The congregation chanted with him. I noticed it was a larger group. Perhaps two hundred people, singing.

I grabbed my jacket and stepped out.

Life was too short to waste it on exploitation flicks and weirdos.

※

Three days later, I had another nightmare.

Light, gentle fingertips fell on my temples, then trickled down my face, neck and chest. Nails raked my arms. I woke to see the woman with the yellow veil. She was on her knees.

She showed me her vulva, spreading it open with her fingers. Yellow, like her skin. An awful, sickly yellow. She pressed her hands, which seemed oily to the touch, against my chest.

I woke up, rushed to the bathroom and vomited.

※

In the morning, I cracked a couple eggs. I stared at the bright yellow yolks, then tossed them down the drain.

I spent most of the morning sitting in the living room, shuffling papers and going over my notes for an arts and culture article. Every once in a while I glanced at the manila folder containing my research on El Tabu. The beige envelope seemed positively yellow. I tossed the whole thing down the garbage chute.

※

Wednesday I dreamt about her again. When I woke up, I could barely button my shirt. I was supposed to go pick up a check for my arts and culture story, but when I reached a busy intersection I caught sight of all the yellow taxis rolling down the street. They resembled lithe scarabs.

A stall had sunflowers for sale. I turned around and rushed back to my apartment.

I sat in front of the television set, shivering.

I'm not sure at what time I fell asleep, but in my dream she was gnawing my chest. I woke up at once, screaming.

I shuffled through the apartment, desperately looking for my cigarettes. I grabbed my backpack, all its contents tumbling onto the floor. My tape recorder bounced against the couch. The play button went on.

I grabbed a cigarette, heard the whirring of the recorder, and then a sound.

It was the movie's soundtrack. It must have been recording the last time I was there.

I was about to switch it off when I heard something.

The cigarette fell from my mouth.

X

Sneaking into El Tabu was not hard. Bums planning on spending the night there did it all the time. I sat in the balcony, my hands on my backpack.

Below me, I counted some three hundred viewers.

The movie began to play. The emperor rode in an open litter. He was headed to a funeral. The funeral of the dark-haired woman. It was a procession. Men held torches to light the way. One could glimpse men and women copulating in the background, behind the rows of slaves with the torches. If you looked carefully, you might see that some of the people writhing on the floor were not making love to anything human.

The emperor rode in his litter and did not see any of this. The camera pulled back to show he was not alone. There was a woman with him. She wore a yellow gown. She began taking off her gown, lifting her veil. It was yellow; the shade of a bright flame.

He looked away from her.

As did I.

I lit a match.

※

I woke up late the next day, to the insistent ringing of the phone.

I picked it up and rested my back against the wall.

It was the lady from the Cineteca Nacional. She said she had that information about the Italian film I had been looking for. It was called *Nero' s Last Days*. They had a print in the vault.

✕

On March 24, 1982, a great fire destroyed ninety-nine percent of the film archives of the Cineteca Nacional. One of the vaults alone kept two thousand prints made out of nitrocellulose. It took the firemen sixteen hours to put the whole thing out.

As for El Tabu, I already told you about it: they made the site into condos after twenty years of the empty, charred lot sitting there.

✕

You are wondering why. I'll tell you why. It was the sound recording. The tape had caught what my ears could not hear: the real audio track of the movie. The voice track.

It's hard to describe.

The sound was yellow. A bright, noxious yellow.

Festering yellow. The sound of withered teeth scraping against flesh. Of pustules bursting open. Diseased. Hungry.

The voice, yellow, speaking to the audience. Telling it things. Asking for things. Yellow limbs and yellow lips, and the yellow maw, the voracious voice that should never have spoken at all.

The things it asked for.

Insatiable. Yellow.

Warning signs are yellow.

I paid attention to the warning.

⋈

I did get that job at the arts and culture magazine. I've been associate editor for five years now, but some things never change. I carry my backpack everywhere, never been a briefcase person. I still smoke a pack a day. Same brand. Still use matches.

Anyway, I've got a very important screening. The Cineteca Nacional is doing a retrospective of 1970s cinema. They have some great Mexican movies. Also some obscure European flicks. There's a rare print that was just discovered a few months ago, part of the film collection of Enrique Zozoya's widow, who was an avid collector of European movies. It was thought lost years ago.

It's called *Nero' s Last Days*.

Since 1982, the Cineteca Nacional has gotten more high-tech, with neat features like its temperature-controlled vaults. But since 1982 I've learned a thing or two about chemistry.

It'll take the firemen more than sixteen hours to put it out.

CEMETERY MAN

She lay bleeding upon her cartridge belts. She could not stand up. The piercing pain in her stomach would not allow it.

Catalina raised her head, squinting.

A man with a long coat, shiny boots and a small leather case – the kind a doctor might use – approached her. Was that their surgeon? She didn't want them to cut her open.

The man paused before her, putting on his hat. She recognized him, all the stories hitting her like a *jicarazo* of icy water at dawn: the Cemetery Man.

Around the campfire, the *soldaderas* joked about the resurrected and the Cemetery Man. Catalina laughed with them. Well-known fighters like La Güera Carrasco, who loved to shoot her gun at the smallest provocation, or Margarita Neri, who was so infamous that the governor of Tabasco hid in a crate when he heard she was approaching his town, were not afraid of the resurrected. Catalina should not show any fear either. But alone, late at night, she did not laugh. She thought of the resurrected lurching across the battlefield and the Cemetery Man, the shadow of his wide-brimmed hat falling upon a corpse.

Catalina wanted to raise her gun and blow his brains out, but her hands trembled and she was only able to scratch the dirt.

The man smiled.

X

Catalina woke to an annoying scraping noise and a sharp pain in her gut. Her head hurt and she winced.

She lay upon a narrow bed, in the darkness. Light filtered through gashes in some curtains.

Her hands felt numb as she flexed them, sluggish thoughts drifting through her brain. She was alive.

Alive … and where?

She pressed her hands against her belly, feeling the bandages beneath her gown.

The scraping returned, loud and irritating. She turned her head.

The resurrected stood in a cage. They had blown half its skull off but a metal plate had replaced the lost bones. The face was badly mangled, stitched together, and the skin was the colour of milk curds. A few tufts of blond hair adhered in dirty clumps to its head. Its eyes were mismatched, shining bright.

The scraping was the sound of the chains against the floor as the creature moved.

Catalina started breathing fast.

"Easy, easy," the Cemetery Man said from behind.

Catalina wanted to speak. The words lodged in her throat. She moved her tongue but could produce no sound.

"Calm down," he said, reaching towards her and placing a hand on her shoulder.

"Don't touch me, you asshole," she slurred. "Damn necromancer."

His face lit up, as though he were mightily amused by her cursing.

"You're very lucky, do you know that? I've saved your life. We wouldn't want to ruin your stitches, would we?"

Catalina gritted her teeth. She did not deign to answer him. He grabbed her arm, tapped at a vein and produced a syringe.

"No," she said, twitching, but he held her arm firmly and slid the needle into her vein.

"Just a tad of morphine," he said. "It always helps to make things better."

He shifted her limbs, like a doll, pulling the covers up.

"You're going to feel much better soon."

"My head hurts."

"Why don't we go to sleep, huh?"

"No," she said, thinking of the resurrected in the corner of the room, staring at her from its cage. What if it broke out? She would not sleep.

Catalina shook her head, her eyes rolling back.

※

Wild dreams. Bizarre images, as if viewed through smoke and fire. The Cemetery Man's wide grin as he looked at her, sharp knife in hand. A pressure upon her skull, so she felt it must burst and she opened her mouth to scream. There was no sound.

Catalina shook, contorting in pain.

※

She woke up and vomited, half of the mess falling upon the bed and the other on the floor. Catalina sobbed into the pillow and did not attempt to move. Footsteps. Strong arms pulling her up.

"Come on, girl."

White, cold tiles against her feet. She saw a chain above her head. They were in the shower. Someone held her up. Someone pulled the chain and cold water rained down on her face.

Catalina shivered as a nurse in a spotless white uniform scrubbed her.

Linen against her skin. Being carried again. She raised her head and saw that the Cemetery Man and a nurse were walking ahead of her. The person carrying her was the tall resurrected she'd seen in the cage.

The resurrected tore soldiers to pieces. They felt no pain. They had no thoughts. They were lumbering, idiotic, murderous machines. She remained perfectly still, not daring to twitch a muscle.

"Set her down."

Covers pulled.

The Cemetery Man brushed the hair from her face. He looked almost kind as he nodded. "Just a little nausea. A side effect from the morphine."

The damn headache. It didn't cease. Catalina moaned. She muttered some gibberish that had no relation to real words.

"Damn it," the man muttered.

He drew his syringe.

No more, she wanted to say. *Oh, no more.*

$$⋊⋉$$

"I want light."

He had been sitting by her side for a good five minutes, but she hadn't been able to bring herself to speak until now. Her throat felt raw and her body ached. The headache, although receding, was still like a splinter in her skull.

"There you are," the Cemetery Man said.

He drew the curtains. The tall windows let the morning sunlight in. He sat down next to her once more.

Catalina turned her head, to see if the resurrected was in its cage. It was. She looked away.

"How are you feeling this morning?"

"Where are we?" she asked.

"An abandoned typhus sanatorium, now my headquarters."

"In what town?"

"Barquilla."

Further than she thought, in the southern portion of the state. An area controlled by the Federales and far from her squadron. They must have travelled by rail. Catalina wondered how the hell she was supposed to make it back to the other *soldaderas,* wounded as she was, without a horse, nor weapons. The man grinned, as if he could read her thoughts.

"You wouldn't last long out there."

He leaned forward and began removing a bandage around her head, slowly taking off the gauze and applying a new one.

"I am Gabriel Mendoza. What's your name?"

He tossed the dirty gauze in a bowl. Catalina did not reply, her jaw set tight.

"I'll call you Adelita then," he said. "Like in the song. Have you heard it?"

"I know the fucking song," she said. "My name is Catalina."

"Cata."

"Catalina," she said.

"Surname?"

"Don't have one."

"Well, Catalina-Don't-Have-One. How do you feel?"

"Great."

"Good. Maybe you'll have some real food today instead of mush," he said, gathering his things and heading towards the door.

"Hey," Catalina yelled, "you're not leaving me alone with that monster are you?"

"He's locked up," Gabriel said with a shrug.

Catalina cursed him and the door slammed shut.

She tried not to look at the creature, but she did. It stood very still in its cage. It was even uglier and more malformed than she thought. She saw that half of its left hand was made of metal and there was another metal plate at its neck. She could picture the machine gun making dozens of holes in the poor bastard's body. Then she thought of Gabriel walking through the battlefield picking the pieces of guts and bone and muscle, sewing them back together and making them walk again.

She pressed her palms against her eyes to stop herself from looking at it.

X

One thing was sure: the Federales ate better than her squadron. It was tortillas with chilli on most days for her. Gabriel brought chicken broth. With real chicken in it. Not just yellow, murky water with the faint flavour of chicken.

Catalina dipped her tortilla into the broth and chewed as fast as she could.

"Don't gorge yourself," he warned her.

"Fuck if I don't," she said.

"You're talking with your mouth open."

"Leave me alone."

He laughed. She thought of slamming the bowl of broth onto his face, but she was hungry. Catalina slurped and ate as quickly as she could.

"You're looking much better today," he said.

"When will I be able to walk?"

"Soon. Don't be thinking you'll run off now that those stitches are healing. There are many soldiers downstairs and they'd be itching to shoot a runaway prisoner."

"Can I sit by the window?"

"No."

Catalina shrugged, handing him her empty bowl and wiping her mouth with the sleeve of her gown.

X

"Where the hell did he come from?" she asked, staring at the resurrected man.

Poncho, the nurse, had brought her injection that day. Aside from the resurrected man and Gabriel, he was the only other person she'd seen since her arrival. Catalina did not know how many people worked with Gabriel, nor did she know how many Federales patrolled the building.

"Brehob?" he asked her.

"Is that its name?"

"Yes. He's a Canadian mercenary. Joined Villa. Gabriel picked him after a battle and brought him back. He thought he might be useful."

Once, on the battlefield, she'd seen a resurrected rip another *soldadera* open and pull her spleen out. Viscera showered the ground. Catalina shot the creature three times, but it didn't go down until a bullet hit its head. She'd developed a healthy fear of the resurrected since then.

She hated the creature, Brehob. The mangled body and the slack, stupid face, tongue lolling out. The thought of being torn to pieces crossed her mind at least once a day.

"He is disgusting. Ah, damn it," she muttered, pressing her closed fist against her forehead as it throbbed. "Hurry."

Poncho slid the needle into place. Catalina thanked God for the morphine. Without it, she feared her head might have split in two. She drifted into the velvet blackness of dreams, punctuated with flashes of red.

She dreamt of blood and the battlefield.

※

"Here. Idle hands belong to the devil," Gabriel said, dumping a book onto her lap.

Catalina stared at it as though it were a live, dangerous animal.

"You said you were bored."

"I said I wanted to sit close to the window."

"This is much better than staring at the sky. You can read and educate yourself."

"I only went to school 'til I was nine. I was a laundress. Not much reading is required."

"How did you end up in a squadron?"

"My dad joined the fight. I travelled with him."

"It seems like a scary proposition."

"I thought I'd be safer as a camp follower. There's money to be made from cooking or washing soldier's uniforms."

She didn't say she was skilled with a Mauser since childhood, when she went hunting with her father. She also didn't say the death of her mother had energized both her and her father, giving them the courage to join the fray. There were soldiers of fortune, of conviction and of circumstance. Catalina fell in the last category.

"But you were part of a female squadron. What happened to your father?"

"How'd you get in bed with the Federales, Cemetery Man?" she shot back.

"I really wish we'd go back to necromancer," he said, shaking his head. "It sounds so much better."

"I'm being polite. They call you El Zopilote, too."

He smiled, a bird of prey's look which seemed very appropriate considering that other nickname.

"How interesting," he said, pausing and rubbing his chin. "My story is very simple, Catalina. I am a scientist, despite the whisperings of the rabble who may claim otherwise. I was researching several interesting aspects of the human brain and body before the Revolution flared up. The conflict has allowed me to put some of my theories to good use."

"You're busy pecking carrion, you mean."

"I am not ashamed of what I do."

"Maybe you should be."

He patted her head, like one might do with a dog or a small child. She flinched.

"As interesting as this conversation is, I have duties to attend to," he said, opening the book to a random word. "There are pictures. You might find it amusing."

Catalina frowned. There were big words in the thick tome.

"Zoology," she muttered, her finger upon the page.

※

Poncho set down the tray next to her and handed her a napkin.

"Why isn't the Cemetery Man here today?" she asked.

"He's busy."

The resurrected wasn't there either, though that was not unusual. Gabriel took it with him often. She preferred it that way. There was nothing more bone-chilling than feeling that monstrosity staring at her with stitched-together, mismatched eyes that seemed to know nothing. Flesh should not be made to shuffle upon earth like this again. Flesh should not give rise to such abominations.

"Is he coming at all?"

"Maybe later."

The door swung open. Another man in a nurse's uniform looked inside, a frantic expression on his face.

"Poncho, come!"

Poncho did not pause to excuse himself. He rushed out, the door banging shut behind him.

Catalina smiled as she realized that in his haste he had not bothered turning the lock. The only time she'd left the room before was when the resurrected carried her to the showers. Not that she had been able to even attempt putting one foot out. But she was feeling much stronger and she had secretly been moving around the room even though Gabriel had warned her she might tear the wound open again.

She'd make some excuse if they found her outside. She'd say she'd had another migraine and went looking for help. They might be upset, but she couldn't miss this chance to inspect her surroundings.

Catalina padded towards the hallway, barefoot – they'd taken away her boots and clothes, the only thing she wore now was a nightgown. She poked her head out the doorway, fearing Poncho would walk back into the room, but the hallway was empty. If there were soldiers on the second floor where she slept, they were not patrolling that day.

Catalina headed down the hallway, glancing at empty rooms. It was very quiet. Very lonely.

The scream made her heart slam against her chest. It echoed down the hallway, eerie in the stillness of the building. Catalina considered retreating quietly to her room. But what if there was another wounded soldier there? Perhaps someone from her same squadron. Catalina inched forward until she reached a door with opaque, milky-blue glass panels. She heard Gabriel's irritated voice coming from inside.

"Didn't I say to gag her? Is it secure this time?"

"Yes, sir."

One of the glass panels was shattered. Catalina looked in.

A woman had been strapped to a bed, face down. Poncho, the nurse and the resurrected were there. She saw a table with odd tools. The smell of chemicals was thick in the air, mixed with the scent of blood.

Gabriel held up a pair of metallic instruments. Something wriggled, caught in the tip of the instruments: an ugly, large, white insect.

"Pull her head up," Gabriel said.

Poncho obeyed. Gabriel pressed the insect against the back of the woman's neck and the thing slipped inside, under her skin.

Gagged or not, the woman let out an inhuman howl which forced Catalina to cover her ears. She stepped back, eyes wide. That was when Gabriel raised his head and saw her.

She ran.

Catalina knew running after you've had a bullet removed from your gut is not the best course of action, but she did not care. She was not going to let him put that thing inside her.

She reached a wide staircase and rushed down, much to the astonishment of a soldier, who stared at her in confusion. She hit him, slammed him against the wall with a loud crack, then kept running down. As soon as she stepped on the ground floor she heard the shots.

Bang! Bang!

Twice. Shot in the back this time.

Catalina fell down.

)(

Catalina lay with her cheek pressed against the pillow, naked, as the Cemetery Man took out the bullets. Delicately, with the utmost care.

The bullets fell, clanging, into a metal dish.

She fell too, into the black maw of an insect.

⚹

"No!"

She jolted up and was surprised to find herself in bed. For a good minute she thought it had all been a nightmare. Then she felt the leather restraints around her wrists.

Catalina arched her back, groaning, feeling a new and fresh ache there.

"You've got a knack for getting hurt," Gabriel said.

"Somebody shot me!"

"And you broke a man's arm."

She recalled the soldier she'd shoved aside. Too bad.

"You keep monsters in this place. You're not putting them in me. You'll have to shoot me again and kill me this time, 'cause I ain't having that!"

"You've already died, you idiot," Gabriel grumbled, his face hovering close to hers.

She tugged at the leather straps, trying to sink her teeth into his neck, like a wild animal.

"Morphine," he demanded.

A nurse, stepping from behind him, handed him a syringe, while Poncho tried to hold her legs down. Poncho was strong, but she was stronger, and she kicked and flailed, sending Poncho stumbling back.

"Brehob!" Gabriel yelled.

The resurrected pinned her down. She stared into its face, his mouth opening and closing like a fish, while the needle slipped into her vein.

)(

This wheelchair had leather straps at the ankles and legs, though they need not have bothered. Catalina sat quiet, staring at the wall.

"They say you are not eating."

She looked up at him.

Gabriel smiled. "We'll force-feed you, if we must."

"What have you done to me?"

"Ah, so you speak at last. Would you really like to know?"

"Yes."

Gabriel reached for the zoology book, flipped through the pages and showed her an illustration.

"*Cymothoa exigua.* A parasitic crustacean which attaches itself to a snapper's tongue. Eventually it causes the tongue to atrophy and replaces the tongue with its own body. I've developed a variation of this parasite. It now resides in your head."

Catalina wanted to scratch her scalp, fearing she could feel something stir beneath her skin. She controlled herself, her hands closing into fists, resting upon her lap.

"Why?"

"The resurrected are good for cannon fodder. They walk into the battlefield, tear a few soldiers to pieces or serve as shields for us. But they can't think. They are strong, resistant and stupid. My most recent experiments focus on making them more intelligent. This parasite adheres to the patient's brain, allowing it to maintain its normal brain functions. It also accelerates your healing process. Think of what that means for a soldier: you always get to come back. Not only come back, but come back better."

Gabriel leaned down. "You should be grateful."

She bared her teeth at him. "I'll kill you."

"You can't. For the same reason that Brehob will never raise his hand at me. For the same reason I can walk by a field full of resurrected without fear: I made you. I own you."

He smiled, lifting her chin. His expression was almost fond.

"You're my best experiment so far," he said, a note of wonder in his voice.

Catalina wanted to bite his fingers and could not. She tasted bile in her mouth and swallowed.

※

She observed her body in wonder as it healed very quickly, even faster than the first time she'd been injured. Benefits of her new condition, Gabriel explained.

The parasite in her head gave her splitting headaches. They increased the morphine. A minor drawback, Gabriel said.

She had nightmares. She dreamt her skin split, pus oozed out, the stench of decay hit her nostrils.

Nothing of importance, just bad dreams that disappear with the morning, Gabriel pointed out.

He did not understand – did not even try to understand – what it meant to be her. What it meant to live and die and live again. The only one who might comprehend was Brehob in its cage, with its dull, empty eyes, staring at her.

It knew.

But she turned her head away from it.

She did not want to be like Brehob.

※

A man came to visit them. His hair was white and he leaned on a silver-tipped cane. He was small and frail, but Catalina noticed the way Gabriel spoke and moved around him and realized the Cemetery Man was intimidated. They spent some time in front of the resurrected's cage, then turned their attention to Catalina.

The old man, who until then had not spoken a word, opened his mouth when he saw her.

"What is your name, girl?" the man asked.

"Catalina," she said.

"How are you feeling today?"

"Fine."

"I've not seen one who can speak," the man said with a nod. "Is she the latest one?"

"Yes." Gabriel said. "She retains all her memories, all her personality. The parasite does subject her to some migraines, some degree of discomfort, but such things are minor. She is our most successful example," Gabriel said.

"But I hear you haven't been able to replicate this success."

Gabriel's face tensed, his eyes filled with an unpleasant sharpness.

"That is a gross simplification," Gabriel said.

"Armando Girat has also been conducting resurrection experiments. He has successfully produced six intelligent resurrected and assures me more can easily be created."

"Girat is not a scientist. His work is that of an amateur, a butcher."

"I have seen his work. It's comparable to yours, Gabriel. We need better soldiers. Soon Villa's rabble will find a resurrection formula for themselves. We cannot lose our edge."

"Villa does not have access to this technology."

"He's brought an American to do some research. A Mr. West. I hear good things about him. Bad for us. I think it would be best if your research were combined with Armando's."

"I will not consent to such a thing," Gabriel said. "I know what he'll do with her. That butcher will cut off her head, steal my parasite and then copy all my work. I'll be left with nothing."

She looked at Gabriel, so smooth and composed on all occasions, now turned ugly, brow frowned, an unpleasant grimace cutting his face.

The old man raised the tip of his cane, pressed it against Gabriel's chest. "I did not ask," he said. "I'll have the girl taken back with me. You'll soon follow, bringing your notes and equipment."

※

Two soldiers came for her in the morning. Poncho injected the morphine, waited a bit, then undid her restraints.

Catalina lay slack against the bed, like a dead fish.

"Let's get you dressed," Poncho said, helping her to sit up.

"Hey, we're running late," one of the soldiers said.

"It won't take long," Poncho muttered. "You think you can drag her around in a nightgown? I've got some clothes here."

"It won't matter one bit."

"Dr. Gabriel said—"

"Yeah, well—"

The soldier didn't have time to complete the sentence. Catalina jumped on top of him, sending him sprawling against the floor and twisting his head in one swift motion.

The other two men stared at her in surprise.

"The doses," Poncho muttered, his hands fluttering as he took a syringe from his coat pocket. "It must not be enough."

The soldier raised his gun at her. Catalina did not give him time to even start squeezing the trigger. She grabbed his arm, twisted it back, bones breaking. The soldier hollered, but she slammed his head against the floor, silencing his screams.

She turned and pointed the gun at Poncho.

"You don't want to die today, do you?" she asked.

He shook his head.

"Give me the needle."

He did. Catalina grabbed it, then hit Poncho on the head with the gun. Poncho blabbered, fell down, and grew silent.

Catalina found the clothes he'd brought for her: a blouse, a skirt and boots. She put them on and took a jacket from one of the soldiers. She also grabbed another gun, a leather holster and a belt.

Dressed and ready, she exited the room. The hallways were empty, just as before. Instead of heading down the main staircase as she'd done the previous time, she moved in the opposite direction: there had to be service stairs. She found them after a little while and hurried down. She came out near the kitchen area and moved towards the stables.

The stables were large but there were only eight horses there. She saddled one horse and spotted a blanket that lay rolled upon a bench.

Catalina had the blanket and was heading back to the horse when a tremendous blow sent her crashing against the floor. She blinked, stunned for a moment, the great outline of Brehob's body blocking the light.

He picked her up with one hand and Catalina tried to kick him, but her blows seemed to have little impact. He punched her in the face and Catalina tasted blood.

"Where do you think you are going?" Gabriel asked.

He was leaning against the stable wall, hands in his pockets.

"Back to my squadron, asshole," she muttered, spitting blood and saliva.

"I don't think you're going anywhere," he said.

Catalina tried to reach for one of the guns, but Brehob twisted her hand and she yelped, feeling the bones crunching.

"Come on, Catalina. It's not going to happen. All you're going to manage is to hurt yourself and then I'll have to put you back together again."

"Go to hell."

Brehob squeezed her hand and she felt the bones breaking.

"Stop it!"

"No, you stop it, Catalina! We both know you need me. You need me to take care of you and of your little parasite. You don't want to be like the resurrected in the battlefield, do you?"

She shook her head.

"Then be a nice girl and stop this."

Catalina ceased squirming. She held her breath.

"Give me her guns," Gabriel ordered. "Then let her go."

Brehob ripped off the holster she was wearing and tossed it to Gabriel. Gabriel held one of the guns and shrugged.

"How far do you think you'd have gotten with only this?" he asked, tossing the weapon to the floor, like a piece of rubbish. Who needed weapons when he had the resurrected to do his bidding?

Brehob set her down and Catalina held her mangled hand, wincing.

"I don't know."

"Not very far. Come here. Let's see what kind of damage we've made."

Catalina shuffled forward. He tilted her face up, brushing her lips, his thumb smeared with her blood.

"Nothing too awful," he muttered, then grabbed her injured hand, looking at the splayed fingers.

As he looked at the broken bones, Catalina raised her good hand and thrust the syringe into his throat. Gabriel opened his eyes wide.

"You can't hurt me," he croaked.

"I'm not hurting you. Just a tad of morphine," she said. "It always helps to make things better."

She pressed a hand against Gabriel's mouth to keep him from speaking and giving Brehob a command. He quickly relaxed against her body and she let him slide upon the floor.

Catalina picked up her gun and pointed it at the unconscious doctor. Her hand shook.

She could not kill him.

Catalina cursed.

She heard the creature moaning. It sounded eerily like a question.

Catalina looked up at its mangled face. The creature looked back at her with its odd eyes, opening its mouth as if it were to speak, but its tongue formed no words. Just the long moan, the clicking of a tongue.

She felt a pinch in her head. The creature opened its mouth in a wide "O" and all she could think about was that time one of them had killed a *soldadera*, and the viscera and the blood, and the stench, and how this thing was just the same kind of abomination.

Catalina squeezed the trigger. Brehob stumbled back and lay resting against a bench.

She moved closer and listened as the tongue kept clicking, words never coming and Brehob looked up at her.

"Bye," she whispered.

She pulled the trigger again, brain matter splattering her.

҉

In the days after, when she rode in search of her squadron, she saw Brehob's face as she went to sleep. She'd killed people before, in battle. One more death was not what kept her up at night.

She thought he was trying to say "please" when she shot him. She thought she'd seen tears in his eyes.

She lay wrapped in her blanket, staring at the stars. Her heavy gun lay next to her good hand. The bad hand was pressed against her chest.

She sensed the little parasite snug inside her skull, and she took a deep breath and she did not know why she'd bothered saying goodbye.

THE DEATH COLLECTOR

There's a murder scheduled in one hour. Mexico City. 1960.

※

Most people would pick another time and place. John F. Kennedy in Dallas. Franz Ferdinand in Sarajevo. Even in Mexico there are more famous sights. The massacre of hundreds of students in the Plaza of the Three Cultures is only eight years away; tanks bulldozing through the streets and the soldiers pouring bullets into the crowd. Forty-seven years in the other direction the streets of Mexico City smell of charred human meat and the screams of the wounded.

Those are large conflicts. Pools of blood spill through the City of Palaces. But the ones I look for are the little deaths. A true collector does not go for the easy, gaudy spectacles printed in bold letters in the history books.

A gourmet of death sniffs for the delicious, the delicate, the more refined crimes rather than clumsy trails of corpses.

No. Mexico City. 1960. Ramon Gay is about to die.

Ramon Gay. He's the true image of a movie star in striking black and white. Mexico's Golden Age of Cinema is grinding to a halt, but there are still actors like Ramon with his sculpted face that cries perfection and his smile that turns women into Jell-O.

Debonair, he struts into the frame with a sense of place, a dignified style. His image burns into the film like a scar upon time. They don't make faces like Ramon's anymore. They don't make murders like his either.

X

My first vacation I went with a buddy to photograph a victim of El Chalequero. A bloodied mannequin staining the pavement. It was so ugly. It was so fake. It was expected: a prostitute in Porfirian Mexico. How passé. Might as well stay home, stare out the window and watch the *narcos* drill bullet holes into a car.

There are ten journalists killed every month – you can watch it online, like a litany. Fifty thousand federal agents can't stem the deaths in the *narco*-north.

Corpses pile at the curb in Ciudad-Estado Juarez and San Simon sits in a corner, a sharp pin in his mouth. There is no elegance in those deaths. They are the deaths of formless, nameless masses. Ugly, stunted citizens of nowhere dying deaths without passion or meaning. Factories of destruction systematically manufacturing bleeding bodies, while the *maquilas* churn out their cheap clothing.

※

It's 1960 in Chilangolandia and in half an hour Ramon Gay is going to park his Dodge at Rio Rhin number sixty.

Ramon, who was in *La Bruja* and *Muñecos Infernales*, piercing eyes elevating a B-movie horror romp into a form of art. Sublime smile in *Eugenia Grandet*. The great laugh. The everything.

No wonder Arturo de Córdova – another leading man, a leading man among leading men – saw that handsome face and fell hard and fast and inexorably.

※

There's two bombings in the subway the week before I leave. I'm not sure if it's *narcos* or cops or someone else on a lark.

Senseless decapitations in Morelos. Heads roll all through the country.

Nothing to admire here. Butcher's work. One hundred years from now no one will remember them; no one will care. They'll be eroded from history while the divine ones, the movie stars, maintain their pace with modernity.

⋊⋉

Fifteen minutes. Evangelina Elizondo and Ramon are coming back from dinner at El Hotel del Paseo. She's an actress and they're both in a play. Her angry ex-husband has been drinking all night, pounding whiskeys at the Terraza Casino.

I can hardly contain myself. I wait around the corner and flip through a newspaper, trying to keep my cool. In the entertainment section there's an ad for an Arturo de Córdova movie playing that day: *El esqueleto de la señora Morales*. It's just premiered. It'll be considered a classic in a few years.

It's the story of a murder.

⋊⋉

The day before my trip a grenade blew up two cops around the corner from my apartment. They cordoned off the block and I worried I wouldn't be able to go on vacation.

My one vacation of the year. All the money stashed away and then some idiot decides to turn a couple of policemen into mush. Everyone in my building had to be questioned.

I was lucky. Someone ratted out the guy on the fourth floor with all the cats. He probably wasn't involved, but he looked like he'd have something to hide. The cops took him away and opened the building again.

I was able to make my departure without further *contretemps*, thank God.

※

The fight begins. The ex-husband finds them sitting in the car, chatting. He is furious. He tries to drag his ex-wife out of the car. Fist crushes bone. Ramon intervenes.

"Stop!"

Five .38-calibre shots in the night.

Later I walk up to Arturo de Córdova as he sits at the table of a popular nightclub. I tell him Ramon has died.

※

I return with a fresh copy of a newspaper rolled under my arm. The headline reads: "No clue of the killer's whereabouts." It will make a lovely addition to my collection.

Passing the fourth floor on the way up the stairs to my apartment, I see that the neighbour's door is open and they're dragging out his furniture. The super doesn't think he'll be back. She confiscates his TV.

It's a city of vultures in an age of carrion. I turn my head and pretend not to see.

Instead I steal a peek at the screen of my camera. The face of Arturo de Córdova stares back at me, caught in the moment I delivered the news. Grief in amber. Precious.

Next year I'll collect another luminary. Another May death. Agustín de Anda. He looked amazing in *Las manzanas de Dorotea*.

I hear cats meowing but I'm far away, lost in halftone smiles of long-dead stars.

THIS STRANGE WAY
OF DYING

1

Georgina met Death when she was ten. The first time she saw him she was reading by her grandmother's bedside. As Georgina tried to pronounce a difficult word, she heard her grandmother groan and looked up. There was a bearded man in a top hat standing by the bed. He wore an orange flower in his buttonhole, the kind Georgina put on the altars on the Day of the Dead.

The man smiled at Georgina with eyes made of coal.

Her grandmother had warned Georgina about Death and asked her to stand guard and chase it away with a pair of scissors. But Georgina had lost the scissors the day before when she made paper animals with her brother Nuncio.

"Please, please don't take my grandmother," she said. "She'll be so angry at me if I let her die."

"We all die," Death said and smiled. "Do not be sad."

He leaned down, his long fingers close to Grandmother's face.

"Wait! What can I do? What should I do?"

"There's not much you can do."

"But I don't want Grandmother to die yet."

"Mmmm," said Death, tapping his foot and taking out a tiny black notebook. "Very well. I'll spare your grandmother. Seven years in exchange for a promise."

"What kind of promise?"

"Any promise. Promises are like cats. A cat may have stripes, or it may be white and have blue eyes and then it is a deaf cat, or it could be a Siamese cat, but it'll always be a cat."

Georgina looked at Death and Death looked back at her, unblinking.

"I suppose … yes," she mumbled.

"Then this is a deal," he said, "Now, have a flower."

He offered her the bright, orange *cempoalxochitl.*

X

That first encounter with Death had a profound effect on Georgina. Fearing Death's reappearance, and thinking he awaited her behind every corner, Georgina took no risks. While Nuncio broke his left arm and scraped his knees, Georgina sat in the darkened salon. When Nuncio rode wildly on his horse or jumped into an automobile, Georgina waited for him by the road.

Finally, when other girls started swooning over young men and wished one of them would sign his name on a dance card, Georgina refused to partner up and join the revelry.

What was the point? She was going to die any day soon, why should she fall in love? Death would come to collect her tomorrow, maybe the day after tomorrow.

She selected the dress that she would be buried in and asked her mother for white lilies at the funeral. She walked around the mausoleum and inspected her final resting place. Morbid scenarios of murder assaulted her. She wondered if she might die struck by a carriage or by lightning, or in some other more remarkable fashion.

This is how seven years passed.

✕

On the seventh year Grandmother died and they took her to the cemetery in the great black hearse, then gathered in the salon to drink and mourn. Georgina was standing by the piano, considering death and its many possibilities, from a bullet to an earthquake, when Catalina came over with a satisfied grin on her face.

"You'll never guess what I heard," she said. "Ignacio Navarrete is going to marry you."

"What?"

"I heard him speaking to Miguel. He's going to ask for your hand in marriage."

"But he can't."

Georgina craned her neck, trying to spot Ignacio across the room and saw him in his double-breasted suit, hands covered in white silk gloves. Reptilian. Disgusting.

"I wish I *would* die," she whispered, angrily, like a bride that has been left at the altar and only now reads the clock and realizes the groom is late.

)(

When Georgina woke up it was dark. A rustle of fabric made her sit up and a man stepped out from behind the thick velvet curtains. He wore a long coat, a burgundy vest and sported a little moustache. Though different in attire, and looking younger than she recalled, she recognized him as Death.

"I didn't really mean it," she said at once, all the scenarios of her own demise suddenly pieced together in her brain.

"Mean what?"

"Today, during the party. I didn't mean I *really* wanted to die."

"You sounded rather honest."

"But I wasn't."

"Then you want to marry that man?"

"No," she scoffed. "I don't want to die either."

"Good. I don't want you to die or marry him."

"Oh," she said.

"You sound disappointed."

"What do you want then? I mean, if you haven't come to kill me."

He produced a bouquet of orange *cempoalxochitls*, his arm stretched out towards her.

"I've come to collect a promise. Any promise, do you recall?"

"Yes," she muttered, uncertain.

"It's a promise of marriage."

Georgina stared at Death. It was the only thing she could do. She was not sure if she should laugh or cry. Probably cry and start yelling for her father. Wouldn't that be the natural reaction?

She pushed her long pigtail behind her shoulder and pressed both hands against the bed.

"I don't think I can marry you," she said cautiously.

"Why not?" he asked.

"You're Death."

"I'm one death."

"Pardon me?"

He grabbed the lilies that were next to her bed and tossed them to the floor, then placed his *cempoalxo-chitls* in the flower vase.

"A few hours ago you were calling for me and now you refuse me."

"I was not ... even if I was ... it's late," she said, reaching towards her embroidered robe. In her white cotton nightgown with the ruffles and lace trim Georgina was practically naked and she didn't think this was the best way to confront Death, or anyone else for that matter.

"Just past midnight."

"Please go," she said, quickly closing the robe, a hand at her neck.

"I cannot leave without the promise of marriage."

"I will not marry you!"

Had she yelled? Georgina pressed a hand against her mouth and immediately feared the maids would come poking their heads inside her room. And what would she say if they found a man in there?

"We have a problem. We made a deal and now I must head out empty-handed, which is impossible in my line of business."

"I'm sorry."

"Sorry," he said and smiled, white teeth flashing, "Sorry does not suffice. No, dear girl. You are indebted to me. You exchanged seven years of life for a promise."

"It isn't fair! I didn't know *what* I promised."

"A promise is a promise," he said, and pulled out his black notebook. "What do you have that you can give? A cat. That is no good. A parrot. Well, they do get to live for a century but I don't think I can stand..."

"I don't want to marry a dead man."

"I'm not dead. I am Death. Particularities, details," he said, scribbling in the notepad. "As you can clearly see your hand in marriage should solve this debt of ours."

"And if I refuse?"

"Let us be reasonable. Would you like to discuss this tomorrow? Shall I meet you around noon?"

Georgina was sure she could hear her mother's sure footsteps approaching her door. Terror greater than death seized her. She wanted the stranger out of her room, out of the house before anyone realized there was a man there.

"Yes, just go," she whispered.

Georgina went to the door, her ear pressed against it. She waited for the door to burst open. It did not. The house was quiet. Her mother slept soundly. She let out a sigh.

Georgina looked around the room. He was gone. The flowers remained, but in the morning they turned into orange dust.

※

Georgina's pigtail was carefully undone and her hair just as carefully swept up and decorated with jewelled pins. She descended the stairs in a tight-waisted blue dress and sat quiet at breakfast, fearing Death would knock at the door and ask to be invited in.

"Will you look at this?" her father said, brandishing the morning newspaper. "It's deplorable. Who does this Orozco think he is? I am telling you Natalia, it is simply deplorable to see such people causing a fuss."

Georgina's mother did not reply. Her father was not asking a question, merely stating his opinion and he expected no replies. He had been a Porfirista before, now he was a Maderista and God knew what he might become the day after. At the table his wife and his two children were supposed to nod their heads and agree in polite silence: father was always right.

"So then, what are your plans for today?" her father asked as he tossed the paper aside.

"I want to get some new dresses made," she replied.

"Nuncio, will you be accompanying your sister?"

"Father, I'm heading to the Jockey Club today," Nuncio said, slipping into his childish, thin voice even though he was a year older than Georgina.

"I want to go alone. I don't need him with me," Georgina said curtly.

Everyone turned to look at her, frowning at the tone she had just used.

"Young ladies do not go out of their houses without proper escorts," her mother reminded her, each word carefully enunciated; a velvet threat.

"This is hardly going out," Georgina countered, knowing well her mother would scold her later for using such a tone with her.

But it would be worse, much worse, if Death were to show up at her home. Perhaps if he found her outside of the house she might speak to him quickly and get rid of him for good, her family never the wiser.

"We'll meet at El Fenix in the afternoon," Georgina said. It wouldn't do at all if Nuncio kept an eye on her all day. "Rosario can accompany me to the seamstress."

※

Rosario chaperoned Georgina, but she was old and tired. Most of the time she would just stay inside the carriage with the coachman, Nicanor, while Georgina hurried into a store. That day was no exception and Georgina went alone up the narrow steps that led to the seamstress. Death, his dark coat spilling behind him, appeared at her elbow.

"Good day," he said, tipping an imaginary hat towards her. "Is today a better time to talk?"

"A little better," she muttered and quickly hurried to the ground floor, where they stood beneath the stairs, hiding in the shadows.

He reached into his pocket and took out a dead dove, trying to hand it to her. Georgina shoved it away. The dove fell on the floor.

"What are you doing?" she asked, staring at the mangled corpse of the bird.

"I thought you'd like a proper engagement present."

"Engagement? You're Death. I'm alive. Isn't that a problem?"

"Of no particular importance," he shrugged.

"Wouldn't you like to marry someone who is dead?"

"Who do you take me for? Do you think I want to go dancing with a cadaver?"

"You don't know me."

"Easily solved. Let us go to a bar and…"

"A bar?!"

"Let us get to know each other somewhere, any-where."

"Nowhere," she whispered, scandalized by the sug-gestion.

"Well, then it is back to the beginning," he said, and took out his notebook and a pencil. "I guess I'll have to take fourteen years of your life then…"

The pencil dangled in mid-air.

"Fourteen?"

"Compound interest."

"Wait," she said. "We can negotiate this."

"Marriage."

"What would you do with a wife? Have little skele-tons and make me cook your meals?"

"Do you like to cook?"

"No!"

"Look, it's a simple matter. Balance and algebra. Duality and all that. Lord and lady. Do you know what I mean?"

She didn't know what to say. She had to talk to the seamstress, had to meet her brother afterwards and maybe Rosario would wake up and wander into the building.

"It would be beautiful," he told her.

Death wove a silver necklace around her neck with vines and birds. The dove fluttered back to life and landing on her hands transformed into a hundred black pearls which spilled onto the floor.

It was all wonderful.

He leaned forward, smelling faintly of incense and copal, of candles burning on the altars. His eyes were so very black, so very deep, and she thought she'd never seen eyes like that; eyes that were dark and quiet as the grave.

She wondered if his lips might taste like sugar skulls.

It was terrifying.

Georgina wept. She tried to hide her face, mortified.

"What is wrong?" Death asked.

"I don't want to," she said.

He frowned. With a wave of his hand the pearls melted away.

"I see. Very well Georgina, perhaps we can revisit our agreement."

Georgina rubbed her eyes and looked up at him.

"I want a day of your life. One day of your heart."

"Just one day?"

"Only one. Tomorrow morning tell everyone you are sick and do not leave your room. I will visit you."

"Yes," she said.

And then he was gone, gone into the shadows, and she ran up the stairs to the dressmaker.

Ж

Georgina told the maids that she felt sick and locked the door. She went behind her painted screen and changed into a simple skirt and blouse. Death appeared early and Georgina sat down in a chair, not knowing what was supposed to happen.

"Perfect. A phonograph," he said, and ran to the other side of the room. "What music do you like?"

"I don't like music. My father bought it for me."

"What about films?" Death asked as he fiddled with her recordings, picking one.

"I don't watch films. I wouldn't be going to a *carpa*."

"Why not?"

"People are rowdy and my mother ... oh, she would go insane if she heard I'd gone anywhere near that sort of place."

"I love films. I love anything that is new and excit-ing. The automobile, for example, is a wonderful method of transportation."

Music began to play and Georgina frowned.

"What is that?" she asked.

"You like it? It's ragtime. Come on, dance with me."

She wondered what she would do if her mother came peeking through the keyhole and saw her dancing with a stranger. What her mother would do to her.

"I don't dance."

"I'll show you."

He took her hand and pulled her up, two steps in the same direction onto the same feet, then a closing step with the other foot. It seemed simple but Georgina kept getting it wrong.

"What?" he asked.

"I didn't think Death would dance. I thought you'd be more … gloomy. And thin."

"So I'm fat, am I?"

"I mean skeleton thin and yellow."

"Why yellow?"

"I don't know. Or maybe red. Like in Poe's story."

"My sister likes red."

"You have siblings?"

"Lots and lots of them."

Georgina, busy watching her feet, finally got it right and laughed.

※

Georgina observed the glass of wine, the grapes and cheese and wondered if she should drink and eat. She recalled how Persephone had been trapped with only six grains of pomegranate. What would happen to her if she ate one whole cheese?

"You're not hungry?" Death said, and lay down on the Persian rug as comfortably and nonchalantly as if he were having a picnic in a field of daisies instead of her room. "What are you thinking about?" Georgina sat very neatly at his side, smoothing her skirt and trying to keep an air of decorum.

"What is your sister like?" she asked, not wanting to talk about Persephone.

"Which one?"

"The one that wears red."

"Oh, her. She's trouble, that one. Hot-headed and angry and crimson. She's definitely not a lady. Or maybe a lady of iron. Tough girl."

"And your brothers?"

"Well, there's one who is like water. He slips in and out of houses, liquid and shimmering and leaves a trail of stars behind."

Georgina tried to picture this and frowned. But she couldn't really see his sister or his brother as anything but skeletons in *papel picado*, pretty decorations for November's altars.

The clock struck midnight, chiming and groaning. The twenty-four hours he had asked for would come to an end soon. Georgina wouldn't see him again. Well, hopefully not until she was a very old and wrinkled lady. Probably a married lady; Mrs. Navarrete with five children and sixteen grandchildren, bent over a cane and unable to dance to any kind of music.

"And then I'll die," she muttered.

"Pardon me?" Death asked, his hands laced behind his head.

"Nothing."

But now that the idea of old age had taken hold of her, now that she could picture herself in wedding and baptismal and anniversary pictures, grey-haired with time stamped on her face, suddenly she wasn't afraid of death. She wasn't afraid of death for the first time in years: she was afraid of life. Or at least, the life she was able to neatly see, the cards laid out with no surprises.

It was horrible.

"I hate my hair," she said and she got up, standing before the full-length mirror and she had no idea why she said this or why the silly chignon made her so furious all of a sudden.

Her fingers tangled in the curls at the nape of her neck and she pulled them, several pins bouncing on the rug.

"I like it," he said, looking over her shoulder and at her reflection.

He smelt of flowers and incense. She thought Death would smell of damp earth and catacombs and be ice cold to the touch. But she'd been wrong about many details concerning Death. Curiously she slipped a hand up, brushing his cheek.

No, he wasn't cold at all but warm and human to the touch.

In the mirror their eyes locked.

"Don't touch me," he warned her. "Or something in you will die."

"I don't believe it," she replied and kissed him on the lips, even if she half believed it.

He tasted sweet.

Death is sweet, she thought and giggled at the thought. He smiled at her, teeth white and perfect and then his smile ebbed and he was serious. He looked at her and she thought he was seeing through the layers of skin and muscle, looking at her naked skeleton and her naked self.

"If you touch me again I'll take your heart," he whispered.

"Then take it," she said with a defiance she hadn't thought she possessed, wishing to die a little.

She slept in death's arms, naked over a rug of orange petals.

2

Georgina had spent the last seven years of her life thinking every day about Death. But now she did not think about him, not even for an instant. This does not mean she thought about life either. In fact, she thought and said very little.

Like a clockwork figurine she rose from her bed, ate her meals and went to mass. But she wasn't really there, instead, she lay suspended in a sleepy haze, resembling a somnambulist walking the tightrope.

Sometimes Georgina would stir, the vague sensation that she'd forgotten something of importance coursing through her body, and then she shook her head. The feeling was insignificant, a phantom limb stretching out.

)(

Georgina rode in her carriage down Plateros. Rosario snored while Georgina observed the men in top hats walking on the sidewalks and the *cargadores* shoving their way through the crowds. She'd gone to her fitting with the seamstress that morning. Her wedding gown. Now she thought about that day almost a year ago when she'd met Death underneath the stairs.

There was something she was forgetting.

There was something else.

But who cared? Wedding gown. Marriage. Life pre-written.

She was getting married in a month's time. Ignacio had bought her a necklace crammed with diamonds from La Esmeralda and her mother had cooed over the extravagant purchase. It would be a good marriage, her father said.

Georgina did not care.

And now she sat so very quietly, so very still, like a living-dead doll staring out the window.

Something caught her eye: a woman in scarlet, her dress so gaudy it burned even among the other prostitutes who were now starting to sneak into the streets as night fell.

Red.

Georgina had been in a trance for twelve months and she had not even realized it. In a little coffin of her own making, Georgina dreamed pleasant dreams. Now she awoke. Apple dislodged, glass crashing.

"Stop!" she ordered Nicanor, and the carriage gave a little jolt.

Georgina climbed out and went towards the woman.

"I know your brother," Georgina said when she reached her.

The prostitute smiled a crimson smile, a hand on her hips.

"Do you? Bastard son of a bitch-mother. Run along."

"No. I mean … I thought … do you know me?"

"He's got a babe on you, has he? Go bother someone else dear, I've got to work."

Georgina was confused. For a moment she thought she had the wrong woman. How could she be mistaken? What could she do? What could she say?

Georgina took a deep breath.

"He is like flowers made of blackness and when he kissed me he tasted like the night."

The prostitute's face did not change. She was still grinning with her ample mouth but her eyes burrowed deeper into Georgina, measuring her.

"What do you want?" asked the red woman.

"Where is he?"

"He's not here. Not now."

"Where is he?"

"What does it matter? You don't want anything with him."

"I said, where is he?"

The woman, taller than Georgina, looked down at her as though she were a small dog yelping at her feet.

"You should head home and marry your rich man, little girl. Forgetting is easy and it doesn't hurt."

"I have already been forgetting."

"Forget some more."

"He has something of mine."

The red death, the woman-death, sneered.

"He'll be at Palacio Nacional in ten days but then he heads north. Catch him then or you'll never catch him at all."

She walked away leaving Georgina standing by the window of a café. Nicanor squinted and gave her a weird look.

"What are you doing talking to that lady, miss Georgina?"

"I'm doing nothing," she replied, and rushing back into the carriage slammed the door shut.

X

When Georgina returned home, her father was very happy and her mother sat on the couch, pale with watery eyes.

"What is it?" she asked.

"The cadets at Tacubaya are up in arms," her father said.

"They're fighting at the Zócalo," her brother said. "They're shooting with machine guns from Palacio Nacional."

And then she thought Death would be at Palacio Nacional in ten days. He had arrived early.

"We'll get Don Porfirio back," her father said, and as usual he was already changing his allegiances, Madero completely forgotten.

)(

It was like a party. A small and insane party. Her father talked animatedly about the events of the day, foretelling the brilliant return to the good old days, to Don Porfirio. But then the chattering grew sparse.

They said several newspaper offices had been set on fire. They said many people were dead. The roar of the cannons echoed non-stop. It got underneath their skin as they sat in the salon. Very quietly, very carefully, the doors were closed, locked with strong wooden beams from the inside.

The electricity had gone out and Georgina lay in the dark listening to the machine guns. They seemed very near.

She pressed a hand against her lips and thought Death must be there, outside, walking through the darkened city.

Her father had the carriage packed with everything he could think to carry. Even a mattress was tied to the roof.

"We're going to Veracruz in the morning," her father repeated. "We're going to Veracruz on the train."

Was there even a train left? The streets were teeming with prisoners that had escaped from Belén and they said the Imperial had been destroyed. Would there be any trains for them?

"We're going to Veracruz in the morning."

"Your hair, pull your hair up girl," her mother ordered, but Georgina did not obey her. It seemed ridiculous to worry about hairpins.

Her mother turned to scream at the maids. Something or the other needed to be taken. Something or the other was valuable and they would have to pack it.

It was the tenth day.

※

On the tenth night Georgina tiptoed down the great staircase and stood at the large front door with the heavy wooden beam in place. Nicanor was sitting with his back to the door.

"What is it, miss?" he asked.

"I need to go out tonight," she said.

"You can't do that. They're fighting."

"I've got to go meet someone. And he won't wait for me," she took out the necklace. "I'll trade you this for a horse and a gun."

The necklace was worth a small fortune. That was what her father had said when he held it up and it shimmered under the chandeliers. Nicanor looked down, staring long and quiet at the jewels.

"I'll be back by dawn," she said.

"No, you won't."

"The fighting has ceased for the night. There's no noise from the cannons."

"What would you be looking for…"

"A man," she said.

"Does he really mean that much to you?"

What a question. What did she know? How dare he ask it? How could she answer it? But there were so many things she never thought she might be able to do, and she'd done them.

"Yes," she said. "Yes, I think he does."

Nicanor took out a pistol.

3

The streets had transformed. The buildings had strange new shadows. It was a different city. Georgina rode through the night and the night had no stars. Only the barking of dogs. She turned a street and a horse came her way, galloping with no rider on its back. The air smelled of iron and there was also another more unpleasant smell: somewhere nearby they were burning the dead.

Closer to the Zócalo she began to meet people, wounded men tottering by, and women. So many women. Tending to their wounded, with *cananas* across their chest and a gun at their hip. She wondered where they came from and who they were fighting for. They might be with Felipe Ángeles, called over to help Madero stall the wave of attackers. They might be anyone.

But he wasn't there and his very absence struck her as unnatural. He must be hiding.

"I am not leaving," she whispered, gripping the reins.

She rushed through streets that snaked and split and went up a hill. The city and the night had no end. She rode through them, not knowing where she was. Georgina believed she might be near Lecumberri or maybe going down Moneda. She saw a car pass her, shining black, and kept riding.

She stumbled onto a wide street where a horse lay on the ground, its entrails spilling out. A group of *rurales* were walking her way. Georgina hid in the shadows, held her pistol and watched them go by.

She thought of death; a bullet lodged in her skull. She wanted to go back home.

"I'm not leaving. Show yourself, coward," she muttered.

And then she saw him, or at last he allowed her to see him, standing in an alley. He had a straw hat that shadowed his face but she recognized Death.

"What are you doing Georgina?" he asked. "You're far from home tonight. Why are you looking for me? We've made our trade."

She dismounted, staring at his face of grey and shadows.

"It was not a fair trade."

"I was more than generous."

"You didn't warn me," she said, and she shoved him against the wall. "I've died."

"Love is dying. Or maybe it's not. It is the opposite. I forget."

"Give me my heart. It's of no use to you."

"On the contrary. It's of no use to *you*, my dear. For what will you do with this heart except let it grow stale and musty in a box?"

"It's mine."

"You couldn't have missed it that much. It's been a year and you haven't remembered it at all."

"It was not yours for the taking!"

"But you didn't want it. You wanted to die and you didn't want it anymore."

"That was before."

"Before what?"

He looked up, the shadows retreating from his face. He had shaved his moustache. He looked younger. A boy, and she a girl.

"I said a day and it was a day. What's fair is fair. You had no right to sneak out with it."

"I warned you," he replied.

"You didn't explain anything at all."

"It was given freely."

"For a day!"

"Sometimes one day is forever."

"You are a sneaky liar, a fraud…"

"Go home Georgina," he said. "My brothers are headed here. Madero dies soon and it'll be very dangerous."

"You're killing him?"

"No. Not I. I'm killing an era. But one of my siblings will. Either way, you'll want to go."

The sound of bullets hitting a wall broke the quiet of the night. Then it faded. Georgina trembled. She wanted to run but she stayed still, her eyes fixed on Death and he looked back at her with his inky gaze. It was he who blinked and turned his head away.

"Persistent, as usual. What then? Oh, fine. Here, take your heart. Bury it in the garden like some radish and see what sprouts."

He opened his hand and a flower fell upon her palm, a bright orange *cempoalxochitl*. She cupped it very carefully, afraid it might break as easily as an egg. She thought it would be difficult to walk all the way home with her hands outstretched, yet she was ready to do it. She'd put it in a box and ship it to Veracruz.

And then, unthinking, driven by impulse or instinct, Georgina crushed the flower against her mouth and it turned to dust upon her lips.

"I hate you," she whispered. "You've changed the world."

"They'll build new palaces, Georgina."

"I don't mean the palaces."

She kissed him, yellow-orange dust still clinging to her mouth. She felt a tear streak her cheek as the heart beat inside her chest once more.

The shadows shifted, turning golden and then swirling black. He rested his forehead against hers, quiet, eyes closed.

"I'm going to Chihuahua. I'm meeting with Villa after this," he said. "It'll be long. It'll be seven years."

"You'll need me."

He opened his eyes and these were golden, like the dawn.

"I do."

He motioned to her horse, which went to them quietly. He offered her a hand and she climbed up, both now clad in the ink of night.

Such is the way of death.

Such is the way of love.

BLOODLINES

Elena flipped the picture of San Antonio de Padua on its head and placed thirteen coins before him. She split a coconut, bathed it in perfume and whispered his name. When neither worked, she phoned Mario. Five minutes later she was yelling at the receiver. My mother was shaking her head.

"She should have given him her menstrual blood to drink. Now there's no way she'll bind him. He's out of love."

"But they've had fights before. He'll come back to beg her forgiveness before next week," I said, and wished it true even though my wishes don't count.

"Not this time."

"Maybe there's something you could do."

"Ha," my mother said.

The screaming stopped. Elena stomped through the living room and went to her room, slamming the door so hard San Antonio's portrait fell to the ground and cracked.

✕

Come morning Cousin Elena's door was open. She stood before her vanity, applying lipstick and humming. She looked especially nice that day, long lustrous hair combed back and high-heeled boots showing off her legs. Elena was the prettiest woman in town, and she knew it.

My whole family was filled with beautiful women. Black-and-white photographs, old Polaroids and even painted portraits testified to a lineage that gave way to the most ravishing beauties in the region. It also gave the women magic and an explosive temper. That temper had driven my great-grandmother to insanity, made my grandmother shoot her husband, and caused my aunt Magdalena to stab her boyfriend on three separate occasions. They got back together after each one of those times, but nevertheless, a stabbing is a stabbing.

I had no beauty and little talent for magic. My mother assured me I was a late bloomer. I didn't believe her.

Short, fat and pimpled, with hair that never stayed in place and crooked teeth decorated with braces: I was potato-bug ugly. Like most bugs, I was in constant danger of being squashed. My cousins did not like me, abhorred the genetic joke that I was, and went to play hand-clapping games by themselves. My schoolmates did not know spells, but didn't enjoy my company either. My only two friends were Paco and Fernando.

The reason why they walked me home some afternoons was so they could ogle my cousin when she danced through the living room wearing her leather miniskirts.

It sucked because Paco was a nice boy with dimples and a good laugh. He always looked through me, like I was the Transparent Woman, you know, that anatomical plastic model I put together the year before.

The people who really looked at me were my cousins Jacinta and Elena. Jacinta was born with a bad eye and the others teased her about it. Her father was of our lineage, which meant she was destined for the *maquilas*: magic can't go through the male bloodline. If you couldn't spin magic, you'd have to bend over a sewing machine and make pants for a few pesos an hour.

Even worse for Jacinta, she was a bastard and we couldn't recognize her as one of the bloodline. My mother had taken pity on her but come sixteen we'd chase her out of the house.

With such low prospects, it made sense that Jacinta would keep me company. It was more difficult to understand why Elena stomached my presence, since she was one of the *brujas chicas*. I think she enjoyed having me run around, doing her errands, crushing beetles for the spells, kneeling in the dirt to pick glass that could be made into bracelets. I was never going to be an important witch, but I made a decent assistant.

Plus I could read Latin, German and French, a feat Elena never achieved. She relied on spells passed through oral tradition, but I liked to pore over the old books and flip through my great-grandmother's grimoire. It gave me a thrill to excel at one thing, even if I could only muster weak spells.

"You going out?" I asked.

"Just heading downtown. I got to do some shopping. I'll be back before supper."

"Can I go with you? I want to watch a movie."

"Some other time," she said, flashing me a smile and putting down her lipstick.

"But if you're heading there anyway…"

The smile turned sour.

"Another time."

I knew better than to push, so I looked for Jacinta. I found her playing behind the house. She was drawing with chalk on the wall, copying the symbols I traced over the bricks. Her marks had no power, so it was a waste of time for her to bother making circles and crosses. But she did it anyway to imitate me.

"Want to ride to the movie theatre on your bicycle?" I asked.

"It's hot outside," she said.

It's always hot. At least in the movie theatre they had air conditioning. Inside our house we only had the fans.

"Come on," I said. "You got money for the ticket?"

"Yeah," she muttered.

"Then let's ride."

"Why doesn't Elena take us in the truck?"

"Elena's gone."

"OK, but I'm hungry."

I sat behind Jacinta while she pedaled. She didn't let me pedal. I didn't blame her; she was afraid I'd damage the old bike. It was the only thing her shit father had left her before he hitched a ride to Guadalajara three years before.

We ate *gaznates* and watched a movie about aliens and then this lady killed them with guns and stuff. It was alright.

When we went out I saw Paco walking down the street, hand in hand with Patricia Espinoza. My heart took a tumble. I thought about Cousin Elena, and how she must feel like she's the Transparent Woman now that Mario doesn't return her calls.

X

For her birthday, my mother took Elena to eat at the Chinese restaurant with the tank full of carp. Jacinta and some of my other cousins came, along with assorted uncles and aunts.

Jacinta and I looked at the carps, tapping our fingers against the glass, while the rest of our family was lost in conversation. They were so busy toasting, making jokes and chatting between themselves that none of them saw Mario and his new girlfriend walk in.

I did. Jacinta noticed and she also stared in their direction.

Slowly, everyone at our table turned their heads and the laughter stopped. Cousin Elena, who was holding her chopsticks in the air, watched the merriment die and her face grew pale. Finally, she turned.

She looked at Mario. Mario looked at her.

Mario stepped out of the restaurant, girlfriend in tow.

I thought Mario was an okay guy, even after he dumped Elena. I owed him one for that time he didn't tell my mom I was sipping booze and smoking dope behind the factory with Jacinta. And overall, well, I thought he was harmless and charming despite his flaws.

But right then, I thought he was an ass for shuffling out like that with a fresh piece of arm candy, just weeks after breaking it off with my cousin.

I'm sure Elena thought the same. Her hand remained suspended in mid-air. Suddenly, she crushed her chopsticks with a flick of her fingers.

The tank behind us exploded, shards of glass flying through the air, water splashing our feet, dribbling across the red and gold carpets. The carp flopped on their bellies. Dying fish mouthed for air.

On an impulse, I grabbed one and rushed to the bathroom. I tossed it into the toilet.

I closed my eyes and wished it would live.

It twitched, then floated up to the surface.

Our magic can never mend broken hearts, nor give life. Spells are for taking, for subduing and stealing. Even if I could cast stronger magic, it would never have worked.

X

Grandmother rarely visited us. She lived down the coast in an old white house that oversaw the beach. There she sat and watched the waves while she strung seashells together and made necklaces. Her eyes were not sharp anymore and her spells had weakened, but she made her necklaces and loaded them with magic nevertheless.

One wonders why, having the power to weave a necklace of death, she once bothered shooting her husband.

Maybe it was more enjoyable that way.

They've got a bad streak, all of the witches in the family.

Anyway, Grandmother came that afternoon, looking like a hermit crab, loaded under the weight of her long grey hair and her years. Jacinta and I pressed our backs against the wall, hiding in the shadows.

We could hear the fan spinning in the living room. Soon we heard Grandmother's steady voice.

Cousin Elena tried to interrupt and there was a slap that echoed throughout the house. She might be one of the four *brujas chicas*, but no match for Grandmother.

I know what Elena did was wrong. We don't flash our gifts in public. In the old days, back when the family was still living in Europe, princes and kings hired our kind to cast spells for them. An invitation would arrive and a contract would be drawn. An infinite number of rules governed family behaviour, including the day when a spell could be cast, as well as the materials employed.

Things changed. Guns and canons made spells with chicken bones archaic. The families sold their services to lower bidders: first merchants, then common folk. The spells, like the families, had lost much of their effectiveness, but when you are paying only a few coins even a mediocre spell will do.

Eventually the families traded Spain for the unknown coasts of America, and like other mercenaries before them, washed up on Veracruz. A few of them went south, off to Argentina and Brazil. Most spread through Mexico.

The luster and weight of the old customs had been lost, but rules remained. Key among them: do not show your magic in public. Spells are intimate things, sewn in private parlours among female relatives.

The slaps continued. Cousin Elena sobbed.

I couldn't bear to hear her crying and I rushed to the living room door, ready to yell at Grandmother. Jacinta pinched my arm and pulled me back.

"Don't," she said. "That's grown-up stuff."

I didn't care what it was. But my valiant rescue was no longer necessary. The door swung open and out walked Cousin Elena. She did not look at us.

⋊

Elena played her radio. She kept the door to her room locked. I knew she was stuffing a dead lizard with ashes.

I knew Elena would blame Mario for grandmother's tongue-lashing and the spectacle at the restaurant, even though he had no direct part in either incident. But I hadn't thought she'd go so far until I saw her catch the lizard using an empty marmalade jar.

"Well, what's the worse thing that could happen?" Jacinta asked.

"Death. Someone should warn him," I said.

"Someone would be stupid."

"Someone would be a coward."

"She could just give him boils on his ass or something," Jacinta said. "Maybe she's not even going to try something real bad."

"You think so?"

Jacinta shrugged. Elena was not going to be content with a mild spell. I would have been, but the power in me was weak; my blood was thin. Elena was a different thing altogether. Elena would kill an ant with a bullet instead of swatting it with a newspaper. She'd nuke it.

I rode the bus all the way across town to the *colonia* where the cars are shiny and there's no broken glass bottles on the walls surrounding the houses. Mario's house was a huge, three-bedroom concrete monster. I felt intimidated just ringing the bell.

The maid let me in and I waited in the game room, which had an enormous TV. It had been fun when Mario invited me and Elena over to watch the TV. He even invited Jacinta one time too.

I felt absolutely rotten when he walked in and smiled at me. On the one hand I was thinking about Elena and on the other well… shit, I didn't want him dead.

"Hey, how's it going?"

"It's going fine," I said.

He nodded. I guessed he was wondering what I was doing in his house. I didn't have time to waste, so I just let it out.

"You've got to get back together with Elena."

"Um, says who?" he asked me, frowning.

"Look, you simply got to. She really misses you and, you know… hey, Mario, you know about my family, right?"

"What, exactly?"

"You know … the thing," I muttered. I didn't want to say witchcraft. We never said it outright to outsiders. Oh, sure. People could whisper all they wanted, but none of the women at the *maquilas* who bought charms to punish their cheating husbands or get back at the greasy foreman making them work two extra hours said the word "witches." Sometimes the adventurous ones, the women who came from the city in their fancy cars, called us "the ladies." Anything more than that was trouble.

Mario stared at me like he had no idea what I was referring to. I wondered if he really was that thickheaded not to have realized Elena was a witch. Maybe he just wanted to believe it wasn't true. Who knows.

"Mario, Elena's going to get back at you if you don't ask her to forgive you and take you back," I said.

"Yeah?" He rolled his eyes. "Did she put you up to this?"

"No! She'd get really mad if she knew."

"It's sweet of you to worry about Elena and me, but we're through. We're not going to go out together again. Besides, I'm seeing someone else."

"You and your girlfriend should get a *cruz de caravaca* and hang it on a red string," I told him.

"Oh, Lourdes, the stuff you say."

A long time ago during the Revolution, a woman in my family transformed her cheating lover into a chair.

Three witches made the man who tried to rape one of them fall off a cliff. An aunt turned into a ball of fire at night and sat on the roof of a farm, cooing for the man who had shot her brother to come out.

This was the kind of outcome Mario would face. You didn't toy with the family. You especially didn't toy with the women. There were new witches and warlocks roaming the north of Mexico, doing work for the drug dealers and the *polleros*, killing each other and squabbling constantly. They didn't mess with us. They knew to steer clear. Mess with the Arietas and you risk your skin.

Mario humiliated Elena. He'd gone out with her for a year and then he dumped her without ceremony. But Elena wasn't like the girls at the *maquila*, sewing blue jeans and shirts; she could sew spells. She could take a needle and black thread and sew a lizard's belly shut. Elena wasn't going to show restraint. She was seething mad and I knew she would kill Mario and his girlfriend.

She was a *bruja chica*, after all.

"Mario, I'm warning you because overall you're an OK guy and I owe you one," I said, thinking about the time he didn't tattle on me and putting my hands in my pockets. "Elena's got a temper and she's really pissed at you. She really, really loved you, do you know that? Other girls, they'll cry it off. Elena will get even. When Elena gets even, you better be afraid. You get it?"

Mario did not answer. He only frowned but I could tell he finally understood.

"Take care," I said.

By the time I got back it was dark. Jacinta was waiting with sweaty palms behind the house.

"You took a long time to come home," she said.

"I went far."

"How far?"

"Mmmmm."

"Did you go to see Mario?"

I fiddled with my plastic watch.

"Hey," said Jacinta. "You went, didn't you?"

"Yeah."

"Are you dumb?"

"Cut it out," I said.

"Elena's going to go apeshit."

It was true. What the hell, I'd already fucked it up so there was no point in moping. I kicked a rock and nodded at Jacinta.

"Damn," Jacinta whispered and bit her lip. "Maybe if we stick together the next few days she won't dare to hurt you."

"Yeah, I don't know about it."

"Or, if she tried to hit you and stuff, I'll go run and get your mom."

It didn't make me feel any better to think about running behind my mom's skirts to avoid Elena's wrath because then I'd have to confess I'd seen Mario. I'd get a good lesson from my grandmother for that. Not only had I discussed family business with an outsider, I'd put a man's safety before my cousin's quest for justice.

Don't get in a witch's path. Especially if you are the weaker witch. If you do, be prepared to face her. That's one of the first things you learn in my family.

X

Two days later, Jacinta and I were reading comic books, sprawled on the hallway floor to keep our bellies cold. I knew I was screwed the moment I heard the click of Elena's high-heeled shoes.

I stood up as she walked down the hallway. Better to face her than begin to run. She'd catch me and it would be even worse.

"You little traitor," she said, jabbing a finger at my chest. "You told him. That lousy coward's left town with his bitch of a girlfriend."

At last Mario had grown a brain. That was nice. On the other hand, Elena was glaring at me.

"Elena, come on," I said, not even pretending inno-cence. "You can't just toss a *maleficio* into the air like that."

"Says who? Mario lied to me."

"What did the girl ever do to you?"

"Oh, so it's that whore that matters instead of me," she said, raising her eyebrows.

Jacinta glanced at me, then back at Elena, not knowing whether to hide or stay.

"No. It's … Elena, it's not fair. It's not right."

"Who the hell do you think you are?"

Elena's nails were long, lacquered and red. She raised them and scratched my cheek, making me wince. Oh, she was pissed.

"I'm going to cast such a spell on you," she said. "I'm going to make your fucking teeth fall out."

"Come on."

She opened her purse and took out the dried lizard, pressing it against my face.

"Lourdes," she whispered to the lizard and I shivered. "Lourdes, Lourdes."

I'd never done a *maleficio* before, but I'd read about it enough times to recognize it and damn, the lizard reeked of concentrated rage and power.

"Don't hurt her!" Jacinta screamed. She gave Elena such a shove that she tripped and fell to the floor.

Jacinta and I froze. We watched in horror as Elena lifted her head, blood pouring from her nose and tears in her eyes.

Elena wouldn't have really hurt me, direct bloodline connecting us and all. But that shove had altered the balance. If she had been pissed before, now she was furious. If she had meant to take revenge on me, now she was aiming for Jacinta. Poor little Jacinta who wasn't even real family, just the bastard daughter of one of the men.

Elena stood up, the lizard cupped in her left hand. She looked like an illustration in one of our old books, a scary convolution of dark, rigid lines.

"One," she muttered, wiping the blood from her nose with her right hand.

There had been a spell next to the illustration. It made me squint when I pored over the letters and tremble because it was not only a *maleficio*, it was my great-grandmother's *maleficio*. They said it was the kind of spell that drove her insane.

"I'm sorry," Jacinta said.

Elena pulled at a thread holding the lizard's belly closed. "Two."

"I said I'm sorry. I'm really sorry!"

"Three."

Elena pulled at another thread. Jacinta was trembling all over and her bad eye, always darting in the wrong direction, had gone white.

I kept thinking of the letters on the book: black on white. Spidery writing extending to the margins and the words so nitid they seemed to flip in my head; turning white upon black, searing the world around me.

"Four," Elena whispered, and a thread of saliva leaked from the corner of Jacinta's mouth.

"Fi—"

Elena gasped. She choked and began to cough. She bent down, pressed her hands against her belly and opened her mouth into an o, spitting a long, black thread. The thread fell to the floor, pooling at her feet.

The words poured from my mouth, loud and blazing white, like the chalkmarks on the walls.

That's the last thing I remember. My mother said she found Elena on her knees and me standing next to her and it took three of the women to stop me from killing Elena.

Which I suppose proves two things: my mother was right about the late blooming and don't get in a witch's path. Especially if you are the weaker witch.

⚬

Grandmother came into the city to see me afterwards and she nodded her head and gave me her blessing. It was all very odd, considering how happy everyone was and how much I'd hurt Elena.

As soon as I could I slipped out of the house.

I found Jacinta behind, drawing stars in the dirt with a stick.

"What's up?" I said.

"Nothing," she muttered and kept on with her drawing.

I watched her trace row upon row of stars.

"You want to read a comic book with me?"

"No."

I scratched my head. "Nothing's going to change, you know."

"It is going to change," she said soberly.

Well, yeah. But I didn't want to say it just like that. Now I would get invited to all the gatherings and I'd never have to set a foot in a *maquila*, not even to sell spells because there'd be better places to hawk my stuff. I could even hex Patricia and twist Paco's dreams until he asked me to be his girlfriend.

"You're going to be just like Elena."

"No I'm not," I protested.

Jacinta gave me a harsh look that made me feel like a cheat.

"Fine, crap," I said, erasing one of the stars with the sole of my shoe. "Look, maybe I will be like Elena..."

"And I'll work at the factory and you'll never talk to me anymore."

"No... look, it doesn't matter. This whole *bruja chica* thing, it's inconsequential."

"Only it's not."

She returned to her pattern of stars, head bowed. At this pace, she'd draw the entire night sky behind our house.

My mouth felt dry and my skin was cold. It wasn't inconsequential and I already felt different. There was a feeling in the pit of my stomach that was half ache and half bliss.

"I'm always going to watch your back," I said. "You'll always watch mine."

Jacinta did not look convinced. She raised her head a fraction, like a deer peering through the trees.

"You sure about that?"

"Yeah."

"Even if we're not bloodline?"

"We *are* bloodline," I told her.

Jacinta smiled real big. She let me ride her bicycle that night while she sat in the back, holding on tight as I circled her mantle of stars.

SHADE OF THE
CEIBA TREE

At night Hun Kay sang lullabies to her little sister with a voice that was like iridescent quetzal feathers, the purest and most wonderful voice Sak Imox had ever heard. Hun Kay's voice could make the fierce jaguar bend its head in reverence.

She sang happy songs, songs of joy and life and flowers and she was, just like her songs, all life and beauty and mirth.

But one morning Sak Imox woke before the dawn to a different kind of song. It was bitter, like the bite of the snake, and it made her shiver.

Hun Kay sat next to Sak Imox and caressed her hair. She was dressed oddly, with many necklaces and bracelets wound around her neck and wrists.

"Little one," she told Sak Imox. "I am sorry to wake you but I wanted to say goodbye, even though mother and father told me I shouldn't."

"Goodbye?"

"Yes. I am going on a journey to meet a great king."

"When will you return?"

Hun Kay did not answer. She kissed her sister's forehead and sang a song about the moon. Sak Imox closed her eyes. It was the last time they spoke.

※

Hun Kay's gift had been in her tongue. She could sing beautifully and had an ease for words which were as sweet as honey when they fell from her mouth. Sak Imox's talent was of a different, less apparent type: she could listen. Her ears were always open. Had she been like the other young ones, caught in the noisy cacophony of play and screams and giggles, she would have been unable to hear the whispers.

"She's with him now," someone said, and Sak Imox raised her head.

Hun Kay was not mentioned, scorched from memory so that any other child would have thought Sak Imox had invented an older sister that never existed. Then again, the other children would not have listened.

"She is under the shade of the ceiba tree," someone else muttered.

Thus even though it was a secret, some sacred knowledge of the village elders, Sak Imox heard and learned about him: the king in the jungle.

Sometimes Sak Imox would dream and in her dreams she saw Hun Kay smile and sing like she had done that morning, long, long ago. When that happened Sak Imox would listen even more closely to the wind and to the water and the earth and the elders and the birds. Soon a word would come and add itself to the puzzle that burned in her mind and word by word she embroidered a story.

There was a being in the jungle and he was feared by the village elders. Some said he was an *alux* but he was not small nor childlike. Instead he appeared as a tall, grown man. Perhaps he was not an *alux*. Perhaps he was something different, much older, much more dangerous.

Sak Imox thought he might be a god. They never said he was a god, just as they never talked of sacrifice and time cycles. But she knew each year a young virgin girl would head into the jungle wearing jade necklaces and bracelets. There she would meet the man they named lord and king and other things, and pledge herself as his wife. Then the man would lay with the woman and afterwards he would kill her.

All this she had learned in secret. The elders who oversaw the event did not divulge the process or its goal. In other villages, in other cities, boys and men were hurled into water-filled caverns and sacrificed to Chac. But this was different. These were young virgin women and the reason for the silence was that it honoured another deity. Most likely, Sak Imox thought, this particular cult was not sanctioned – perhaps it was even forbidden – by the *kuhul ajaw*.

Whatever the reason, a code of silence had taken root among the villagers. Young girls left the village yet nobody spoke of it or against it. Nobody said: the bones of our daughters rot under the ceiba tree. But she knew. She knew the truth. Just like she knew Nicte Ha was the next girl who would venture into the jungle.

))(

"It will be soon, will it not?" Sak Imox asked her cousin one day as they were doing the washing.

Nicte Ha looked up at her.

"What will be soon?" she asked innocently.

"How did they pick you? When were you told?"

"I do not understand," Nicte Ha said, but her eyes evaded her.

"I know about the king that sits beneath the tree," she said.

"We are not supposed to talk of it."

"Nobody is listening."

They were atop some rocks which emerged from the water hole, away from some of the other women who were also washing their clothes that morning.

Nicte Ha hesitated for a moment, then she leaned forward and spoke in a whisper.

"They said in a week I shall bid goodbye to my parents and go to meet him."

"What else?"

"Not much else."

"Will you go?"

"I have to. They'll see to it."

"You could run away."

Nicte Ha shook her head.

"Where would I go? They'd find me," she muttered.

One of her elder cousins was approaching them and Sak Imox spoke quickly.

"Meet me tonight and we will talk more."

"What is there to talk about?"

"Much."

X

Sak Imox and Nicte Ha met before dawn. Her cousin handed her the necklaces and the bracelets.

"They'll be very angry," Nicte Ha said, biting her lip.

"They would not harm you," Sak Imox said. "It's a fair trade."

Perhaps they would even be pleased that Sak Imox had volunteered, had willingly taken the other girl's place.

Nicte Ha embraced her. Sak Imox pushed her gently away and moved towards the narrow road that went through the jungle. As she walked the sky coloured a bright red and yellow, morning blooming all around her, and Sak Imox felt the wind caress her cheek. A curious wind.

An omen, a mark or a welcome. She was not sure. But she knew the villagers would never venture after her and into his realm. They would not dare.

X

The road had once led to a great city. But the city disappeared; it was destroyed, abandoned and forgotten. Nothing remained of it except the narrow road and the village by the road, poised at the edge of the jungle. And he, of course. He remained although Sak Imox could not say if he had been part of the city. He might have preceded it. He might have sprung up after its fall, like mushrooms sprouting from the earth.

Sak Imox followed the center of the path and kept her eyes on the road ahead. Sometimes a bright green bird would flutter above her head and she felt its eyes were too smart and bright for a normal bird. But this did not deter her.

Neither did the night. She had known it would be a two-day journey and she did not shiver in apprehension as she curled down in the middle of the road. She did not fear the jaguar might devour her.

The noises of the jungle intensified with the darkness and the leaves in the trees shook, warning her.

"Fly, flee," said a bat, flapping its wings. "There is danger down this road."

"I seek my sister who is lost," Sak Imox told the bat.

"I have not seen her when I've flown through the night."

Sak Imox thanked the bat and curled up tight, like a child in the womb. She slept upon her bed of dark earth and dreamed of a huge tree. Bones surrounded the tree and tangled under its roots; some white and others yellow. Some were cracked, others nothing more than powder upon the ground.

She found her sister's skull and picked it up. She kissed its forehead lovingly and nursed it like a child. The skull wept against her breast and sang a broken song.

※

On the evening of the second day she found the ceiba tree. It was huge, with buttressed roots taller than Sak Imox and a wide canopy above her head. Pretty, tiny flowers streaked the ground white around it. There were no bats lingering near it, nor monkeys or eagles. No life stirred within the tree and when she asked a question, the tree would not answer. Thus she knew she had reached her destination.

She sat down, her head against the grey roots of the tree. There was nothing for her to do now but wait.

God or monster he would come to her. She slept, and on this second day her dreams were peaceful, brimming with her sister's lullaby.

※

Fingers ran through Sak Imox's hair. She opened her eyes and stared into the face of a young man. She was startled by his handsome profile, the serpentine grace of his smile.

"Do not be afraid," he said.

She stood up and moved away from him, an instinctive gesture. Night cloaked them and in the darkness the tree had turned the colour of silver. He wore robes made with a piece of the night sky and carried an obsidian dagger at his waist.

"Although there is not much space for fear in your heart, is there, brave girl?"

"What do you mean?" she asked.

"You are not the woman who was intended for me," he said, with a voice that made her weak and drowsy.

"I have taken my cousin's place," she whispered.

"Very brave. Very noble. Or perhaps very selfish."

She took a step towards him. Her body seemed to have a will of its own, it flew on invisible wings. The jungle whispered words she did not know.

"What do you mean?"

"Perhaps you thought yourself more suitable for this task. More beautiful and more intelligent. A better match for me, a better bride. Has vanity pulled you to my side?"

"Curiosity."

"How so?"

"I wondered," she said, slowly. "I wondered about you."

"Did you?" he asked, and his eyes shone with the silver of the tree.

Closer she went, drawn by the mysterious tone of his voice. Such a beautiful, melodic voice. It was made of jade. It was the sun and the wind. It was everything in the world erasing the ground beneath her feet. It was love. It was desire.

She burned for him, a small ember that wished only to be consumed. She would gladly kneel at his feet, offer herself in sacrifice. She would be anything he wished her to be.

"Take my hand," he said. "Take my kiss."

It was then, only then as she was a step from him, that she heard that other note in his voice. Perhaps no one else could have heard it but she did. Her finely trained ear fixed upon the hard, sharp edge of it.

She had thought his voice was translucent, it was joy and love, yet she discerned beneath the layers of beauty the subtle murmur of death and the splash of blood against the earth.

She stood before him, a girl with no shield except the strength of her resolve and no weapon but her wits.

"Are you a god or a man?" she asked.

His hand brushed her shoulder.

"In the village they all whispered different stories and none could say what was your true nature."

"I am many things."

"But all things have one final truth."

"You think me a god?" he said as he circled her.

"I do not know."

He smiled and bent down to kiss her. She moved her head and his lips touched her cheek instead of her mouth. His sorcery was still thick around her but it had been momentarily torn and she was able to speak lucidly, to raise her eyes to him with impudence.

"You demand a sacrifice."

"There is a requirement, a need, for an offering of blood," he said.

She thought of the knife, of her throat arched against a black blade but she did not shudder. She sensed that fear as much as desire were his tools. He would not pry her open so easily.

"May I make a demand of my own? May there be a present for the bride?"

He was amused, his mouth shaping into a wide grin.

"What do you want?"

"My sister's bones."

He kept smiling. His face did not change. Yet she thought the air grew a little colder and the night which had been full with the music of insects hushed itself.

"What kind of present is that?"

"It is the only thing I ask of you."

"And why would you want such a thing?"

"To gaze at her one more time."

For a moment she thought he would refuse her. Perhaps no one had ever asked anything of him. Perhaps he would kill her for her brazenness. Nevertheless, she sensed it was not so simple, that he must follow the right steps.

"Very well. A present, for a special woman, a special bride."

He placed a hand against the silver trunk of the tree and whispered a word. The roots moved, uncoiling like snakes, and from the earth the skull and bones emerged, gleaming white, and lay there at his feet. She leaned down, touching the brittle shell that had held her sister's mind.

"I am with you," Sak Imox said. "Sing me songs again."

She rose and turned to the man and before he could make any demands she removed her dress. She displayed her body defiantly and when he smiled, a different smile this time, she did not blush. Nor did she shudder when he cupped her face, ran his hands down her legs and pressed her back against the tree.

But the tree did shudder. It beat like a heart while the man looked at her with silver eyes, shining and deep like the *dzonot,* but she buried her face in his neck, evading the bottom of those waters. When he took her there was the requisite pain and blood upon her thighs, but she did not scream, biting down on his shoulder instead. And when he whispered to her with a sorcerer's voice made of stars, binding her with each word, she thought of her childhood and her sister singing to her and his chains melted away. Thus she fell into darkness but was never swallowed by it.

X

Her sister's bones sang a bitter song and woke Sak Imox before the dawn just like she'd done ten years before. Sak Imox stood up under the shade of the ceiba tree and glanced at the naked, sleeping man at her side, stretched out with his hair covering his face. Close to him lay their discarded clothing, the knife and the jade ornaments.

Morning would break soon and his silver eyes would open and he would place the jade necklace around her neck once more, the dress upon her body. He would hold her hand and kiss her cheek like a most beloved bride and then he would raise his knife.

Innocent blood twice shed, in darkness and in light.

But of course he had not thought, had not considered, Hun Kay's song and Sak Imox's finely tuned ear. And though Sak Imox should not be awake, caught in the spell of the man, her eyes were very much open.

Sak Imox grabbed the man's knife. The ceiba tree rippled, an unpleasant tremor that almost forced her to drop the weapon, but her sister's bones sang another song – the lullaby of their childhood – and the tree was bound tight.

The bones continued to sing as Sak Imox sliced the man's throat. Blood soaked the ground. Blood dripped down Sak Imox's hands and the man's silver eyes snapped open. He tried to speak, perhaps to weave his magic around her, but no sound could escape his mouth.

He reached out to her. Sak Imox pressed a bloody palm against the trunk of the tree and the tree groaned. It twisted its trunk, a snake contorting in agony. Cracks appeared, flowing up, and the tree shattered into a thousand grey pieces until there was nothing but dust and then the dust was blown away by the wind so that nothing remained.

When the last speck of the tree had been scattered the man's eyes fell shut and he grew still.

Sak Imox leaned down and gathered her sister's bones. Then she walked away, towards the place where the sun was gnawing the sky.

SNOW

The decapitated snowman stood by the front of the dorm. Its head lay at its feet. She remembered a random comment a student had yelled the night before, during the party: the end of the world is now.

Emma tied the scarf around her neck and trudged towards the dining hall. It was almost empty. The majority of students had already left. The remaining ones were busy hauling their dirty laundry off campus for their mothers to wash during the winter break. Emma had planned to spend Christmas break with Colin, in Los Angeles. But they'd broken up before finals.

Instead of snapping pictures of palm trees she stirred her bowl of cereal with a plastic spoon. She waited until the cereal became soggy and ate slowly. When she was done she unzipped her backpack and took out a yellowing paperback with marble pillars on the cover. She was determined to fill her days with homework and reading.

Half an hour later one of the dining hall attendants told her they were closing down.

"Storm's coming," he told her.

Emma nodded and grabbed her things. When she stepped outside the sky looked crisp and clear and there was not a hint of snow.

⚹

The wind started picking up before midnight. Emma glanced out the window. Snowflakes streaked the sky, growing in size. The trees rattled against the old house-turned-dorm. The floorboards moaned.

Emma put the book aside and turned off the lights. She dreamed of giant penguins marching across an ice plain and woke up early.

She peeked outside, eyes fixing on the snowman she had mutilated; its head was now buried under the fresh snow. Emma went down to the communal kitchen and placed the kettle on the burner. She had tea and cookies, then put on her jacket, laced her boots and decided to pay Sophie a visit.

Sophie's dorm was on the other side of campus and Emma wondered if she might be able to get a lift. But no one was out that morning.

When she reached Sophie's dorm she saw the front door had been left open, propped with a rock. Snow as fine as powdered sugar had settled on the carpet, reaching the couches and the television set. Judging by the amount of it, the door must have been left open the whole night. The resident assistants would have a fit when they came back to damaged furniture.

Emma went up the stairs and knocked on Sophie's door. Sophie did not answer.

Emma frowned. She had not thought to phone Sophie before coming over. When they'd spoken at the party, Sophie had confirmed she was going to remain on campus. Had she left? Emma scribbled a note on Sophie's whiteboard using the red marker attached to it with a frayed cord. The letters were thin, spidery loops. She underlined a word.

Emma walked back to her dorm, following the paths by memory instead of sight because they were hidden under the whiteness.

※

Emma sorted socks and folded clothes. She read and waited for Sophie to phone. There were no calls. When night fell she turned on her television set and saw only static. She'd tell the campus cops about the cable in the morning, when they did their rounds. She couldn't be bothered to call them right that instant.

Emma opened a can of Vienna sausages and ate it by the window, watching the trees bend and shake, the snow swirl and fall. The snowman she'd built with Colin just a couple of weeks before was disappearing little by little, swallowed by the cold.

She thought about the spring of the previous year, when they'd met, and the charming way in which Colin massacred French during their language labs. Then she frowned, remembering how he'd looked with his mouth all over Claire Anderson at the party. Emma hadn't wanted to go to the party, but Sophie dragged her and told her it would be fun to play beer-pong and have Jell-O-shots. But Colin had been there, fully in the throes of Rebound 101, and all Emma did was sit in a dark corner, listening to a random guy babble about weather patterns until eventually he told her the end of the world was now. Or nigh. Or some other bullshit and Emma excused herself, walked back to her dorm and mauled the snowman, flinging off its head.

Emma looked at the pale sausages, the colour of frozen fingers. Or maggots. Three hundred calories, almost two hundred and fifty of these in saturated fat. Battered meat pushed into a sieve and reformed. It tasted like crap but it required little effort and there was a certain pleasure in sinking her fingers into the can and fishing for the sausages. Her indifference as she ate and stared at the snow was a quiet statement to the harsh winter: you can maul the house with this storm and I can eat my canned food.

So she ate and nodded as the house shivered.

❊

Emma noticed the tracks going around the house and wished she'd risen earlier. The campus cops must have done their rounds already and wouldn't come back until the next day. If they did. She'd pulled out her hand-crank radio from under the bed earlier – legacy of her days as a Girl Scout – and listened to the news. They were talking about a storm, a big one, headed her way. Storm of the century, someone had said, and if it was *that* bad then she doubted the cops would be doing their usual rounds, winter break and a lonely campus and all.

Emma placed her hands in her pockets and contemplated walking over to Sophie's dorm. It was very chilly and the snowdrifts looked high, plus she had no idea if Sophie was even there. She might have gone to town to get supplies in preparation for the big one. She might be sitting at Gino's, eating a warm split-pea soup, with a bag full of that horrible granola cereal she liked to buy. For a minute, Emma considered going into town. Having a coffee, eating a slice of pie; these things might lift her spirits. But Emma didn't own a car and walking into town took half an hour. In good conditions. In this snow, it would take twice as long and it wouldn't be worth the effort.

Emma stopped by the entrance, looking for their snowman. Somebody had smashed it into a pulp and shoved the remains of its lumpy body onto the ground. The murder weapon – a tree branch – had been abandoned next to the corpse. She was alone in her dorm but Dyer Hall was just across the street and some of the men there had egged her dorm that Halloween. Those pranksters wouldn't think twice about beating the crap out of a snowman.

The thought of reckless young men running around campus, stomping on snowmen, had an unpleasant edge to it but she was also glad the snowman was completely gone.

Emma stepped back inside. She phoned campus security, but got the voice mail at the first try. She left a brief message about the cable, then looked for her old pair of skates.

There was a pond near her dorm, a little opening of water where the ducks and geese gathered in the spring. Sometimes, during the winter, drunk students would cut across the pond, running over the ice, and fall down, injuring themselves. They said a girl had committed suicide there a hundred years before and some talked about ghosts, but Emma had seen none.

Emma put the skates on and traced circles with the blades, tattooing the ice with foreign words, lines, shapes.

❊

She thought about giant penguins as she stirred the mac and cheese. The hand-crank radio played classical music, the kind her nana liked to play on Sundays before the cancer gnawed her entrails.

She pictured the penguins marching in a straight line, in the snow, underneath a starless sky.

In her room, the phone rang.

Emma bolted up the stairs and grabbed the receiver.

"Hello?" she said.

There was a garbled word – more like a gurgle – and the line went dead. Great. She had probably missed Sophie. Instinct, though, told her it must have been Colin, not Sophie.

Colin. With the curly hair at his nape and his wicked half-smile. Colin at the party drinking his beer, laughing, kissing Claire while Emma listened to the boy who talked about the apocalypse.

Emma placed the receiver back in its place and went to the kitchen, to her half-burnt mac and cheese and the silence of the small dorm.

※

She read until late even though the words slid into the darkness and the book did not make sense. When she reached to turn off her lamp she looked out the window and saw someone standing across the street, looking at the sky. It was too dark and too snowy to make out who this was, though she pegged this for one of the kids from Dyer Hall; perhaps the very one who had taken care of her snowman.

She squinted, trying to see if there were any lights on over at Dyer Hall. The house across the street seemed to be painted with blackness, nothing but a shadow sticking out in the snow.

※

She didn't think it would be that bad of a winter break, but the snow was coming thick and strong. By the time Emma had breakfast she was reconsidering stepping outside. But she wanted to see if Sophie was around and with the phone lines gone to hell she must walk to her place.

Emma grabbed her mittens, pausing at the door to stare at the snowman that had replaced her old one. Well, calling it a snowman was a bit of a stretch. It was just a mound of snow, piled high, with no definite form. The student from Dyer Hall who had shaped this snow creation – for it must have been the one she had spotted the previous night – had not spent much time perfecting it.

Emma went down the hill, watching her footing. The snowdrifts were getting perilously high and the wind chill was unbelievable. By the time she walked by the library, she was ready to call it quits. She paused near the library's steps – or where the steps would have been, had they not been covered in snow – and noticed the front door was slightly ajar.

Emma frowned. The library, just like the dining hall, was locked during Christmas break. She wondered if the cops were doing their rounds.

Emma peeked her head inside the library. The lights were all off. The service desk was empty, the books all neatly lined on their shelves. Emma quietly closed the door behind her and went out again.

Her breath rose in a puff and she thought about this documentary she had watched as a child, about Antarctica. White cliffs rising behind a group of men. Explorers in a black-and-white film reel, with parkas and sled dogs and their blurred faces before the old camera. The narrator talked about the Nordenskjoeld's Giant Penguin, now extinct, and the child Emma wished she could become an explorer of secret lands but Billy – who sat in front of her in Miss Ollin's class – said there were no secret places left.

※

Emma skated on the pond, digging the blade into the icy surface. For her amusement, she recited Latin names she had picked from biology textbooks and traced circle upon circle.

The wind, when it rustled the trees, paused to whisper her name.

Ж

The radio was calling it the storm of the century. Emma watched the wind whipping the trees, listened to its howl as it swept ice and snow across her window. Nearby the ocean raged, rising and licking the land.

She wondered if it was century or decade or just another exaggeration.

She wondered if Colin was in California, baking under the sun, or closer by, in the arms of Claire Anderson. She pictured them together, sharing a blanket, freezing to death. Pale limbs shimmered under the light of the moon as the storm broke down their doors, invaded their room and swallowed them whole.

She pictured Sophie sleeping beneath the pond, body encased in ice, and smiled because Sophie had known about Claire and had not breathed a word to Emma. Sophie who had been her friend. Sophie who thought all wounds can heal with two rounds of Jell-O-shots and the toss of a plastic ball into a beer cup.

Emma found a pack of cigarettes in her room. She did not recall smoking. She lit a cigarette and the lights went off. Emma sat in the darkness, flicking the lighter on and off. On and off.

Ж

The clock said it was morning but there was no light. All Emma glimpsed from her window was the snow accumulating higher and higher, the sharp shards of ice dangling from the roof.

She cranked the radio and there came a garbled report. River. Destroyed bridges. Submerged towns. Police. Mobilized. Storm.

The radio announcer said the end is nigh.

Emma nodded her understanding.

Across the street she saw pale figures emerging from the snow. Penguins, the size of men, walking in a straight line.

She remembered staring at the penguins in the zoo, wanting to touch them. Wanting to see if they carried a piece of ice inside their heart. She remembered the old film with the explorers. The white chasm. The pale slopes extending to forever.

Emma put on her parka but she did not bother with gloves or shoes. The snow crunched beneath her bare feet.

She followed the penguins, her fingers brushing their sleek bodies. They were warm to the touch, like the bread her nana used to bake.

Ahead of the penguin column, by the sea, she could glimpse tall towers carved out of ice; the secret place she had sought her entire life.

"Mexican by birth, Canadian by inclination," Silvia Moreno-Garcia is the author of eight books, and has edited the critically acclaimed anthologies *Dead North: Canadian Zombie Fiction* and *Fractured: Tales of the Canadian Post-Apocalypse* (Exile Editions). Silvia is a publisher of Innsmouth Free Press, as well as being a columnist for the *Washington Post*. She holds an MA in Science and Technology Studies from the University of British Columbia. *Gods of Jade and Shadow* was the 2020 winner of the Sunburst Award for Adult Fiction.